995

BODY
TRAFFIC

BOOKS BY STEPHEN DOBYNS

POETRY

Body Traffic (1990)

Cemetery Nights (1987)

Black Dog, Red Dog (1984)

The Balthus Poems (1982)

Heat Death (1980)

Griffon (1976)

Concurring Beasts (1972)

NOVELS

Saratoga Hexameter (1990)

The House on Alexandrine (1990)

Saratoga Bestiary (1988)

The Two Deaths of Señora Puccini (1988)

A Boat Off the Coast (1987)

Saratoga Snapper (1986)

Cold Dog Soup (1985)

Saratoga Headhunter (1985)

Dancer with One Leg (1983)

Saratoga Swimmer (1981)

Saratoga Longshot (1976)

A Man of Little Evils (1973)

BODY
TRAFFIC

Poems by
STEPHEN DOBYNS

VIKING

VIKING
Published by the Penguin Group
Viking Penguin, a division of Penguin Books USA Inc.,
375 Hudson Street, New York, New York 10014, U.S.A.
Penguin Books Ltd, 27 Wrights Lane,
London W8 5TZ, England
Penguin Books Australia Ltd, Ringwood,
Victoria, Australia
Penguin Books Canada Ltd, 2801 John Street,
Markham, Ontario, Canada L3R 1B4
Penguin Books (N.Z.) Ltd, 182–190 Wairau Road,
Auckland 10, New Zealand

Penguin Books Ltd, Registered Offices:
Harmondsworth, Middlesex, England

First published in 1990 by Viking Penguin,
a division of Penguin Books USA Inc.

1 3 5 7 9 10 8 6 4 2

Page xi constitutes an extension of this copyright page.

LIBRARY OF CONGRESS CATALOGING IN PUBLICATION DATA
Dobyns, Stephen, 1941–
Body traffic / Stephen Dobyns.
p. cm.
ISBN 0-670-83088-7
I. Title.
PS3554.O2B64   1990
811'.54—dc20   90-50003

Printed in the United States of America
Set in Baskerville
Designed by Kathryn Parise

CONTENTS

Acknowledgment is due to the editors of the following publications in whose pages some of these poems first appeared.

The American Poetry Review: "The Belly," "Black Girl Vanishing: Detroit 1970," "The Body's Weight," "Careers," "Expansion Slots," "The Proof," "Feet," "How You Are Linked," "Laughter," "Receivers of the World's Attention," "Traffic"

Antaeus: "The Body's Curse," "The Body's Hope," "Desire"

Boulevard: "The Future," "Toting It Up"

Cutbank: "Walls to Take Up, Walls to Take Down"

The Gettysburg Review: "The Music One Looks Back On," "Summer Evenings"

Indiana Review: "The Body's Repose and Discontent," "Canto Hondo," "How It Was at the End," "Surprise," "Tongue"

Ironwood: "Folk Tales," "No Map," "Shrill," "How Could You Ever Be Fine?"

Onthebus: "The Double," "In a Row," "Morning News"

The Paris Review: "The Body's Strength," "Eyelids," "Fingernails," "Slipping Away," "Sweat"

Ploughshares: "Boneyard," "The Children," "Confession," "The Day the World Ends," "Delicious Monstrosity," "What You Should Have Thought About Earlier"

Poetry: "Adam," "Brink," "Freight Cars," "Long Story," "Rootless," "Thoughts at Thirty Thousand Feet," "Utopian Melodies"

Special Report: Fiction: "Shaving"

The Times Literary Supplement: "Hospital Waiting Room," "Skeleton"

Virginia Quarterly Review: "The Body's Journey," "The Body's Joy," "Invasions," "Spleen"

BODY
TRAFFIC

THE BODY'S JOURNEY

Born, it's not good for much, a vehicle
stuck on its top, spinning its tires,
a pink VW Beetle or something resembling
a turtle. But it's cute so we keep it.

Soon it gets the hang of things and starts
to travel—first on its pudgy belly, then
on its beefy knees, until dangerously,
stubbornly, it wobbles along on two legs.

After that there's no holding it back—
think of the jazz it is able to dance
and the odd machinery it learns to drive:
unicycles, bathyspheres, spaceships,

as well as people. That really
is our main system of forward progression,
like a lemming or salmon—Toot, toot,
hey buddy, you're blocking the road!—

climbing over the bodies of all the folks
around us, until one can imagine a humungous
Himalaya of human flesh; and what a struggle
to this journey—a foot in this one's face,

one woman dragging herself up by the long
black tresses of another, an old man slamming
his cudgel against another old man's
bald spot, thousands scrambling to the top,

*   *   *

as millions of others sink within. And even
the losers, those near the bottom, keep
stamping on the rascals beneath them, just
to make sure they stay put. One wonders

at the fellow at the very bottom—saint or jerk,
cripple or coward—but perhaps there is no
actual bottom, just as one can't imagine
an absolute top, only fog at either end

with constant motion in between, everybody
frantic and all getting faster till one by one
they stumble from the crowd and each person's
private death greets him with a peck on the cheek.

But even then they keep traveling as death
climbs aboard each one, straddles each one
like a man paddling a canoe up a river and they
push off toward that place which nobody conquers.

Willows dabble their green hands in the water.
What memories alternate with what regrets,
what wistful hankerings, as the paddle repeats
its calming stroke and a loon warbles its cry?

THE BELLY

The belly puts on a bright red wig.
It puts on earmuffs and a pair of glasses.
It puts on a hat of crushed felt.
The belly thinks it's a brain.
It fits itself with a set of teeth.
I'm hungry, says the belly, I want more.
The belly decides to see the world.
It begins to travel. With its
perfect disguise it is invited everywhere.
The belly attends the meetings of bankers.
With its new mouth it says,
In my most considered opinion . . .
In its belly heart it says, I like sweet things.
The belly attends the meetings of university professors.
With its new lips it says,
When one considers what is reasonable and just . . .
Deep inside it says, I like soft things.
The belly talks to a beautiful woman.
With its new teeth it says,
There is much truth in your argument . . .
In its belly heart it says, I want your cunt.
The belly travels and travels.
Wherever it goes people are impressed.
How smart it is, how terribly kind.
When the belly was a belly, it was always hungry.
Now that it's a brain it has gotten very fat.
What are the loves of the belly?
Anything vulnerable and unprotected,
anything desired by anyone else.
What are the fears of the belly?

Sharp things, things with teeth, bigger bellies.
What are the dreams of the belly?
Floating through space the belly comes to the edge
of the universe and sees the alternative universe
floating toward it. In fact, it sees itself
floating toward it. The belly and alternative belly
both open their mouths very wide.
Starlight flickers across their steel teeth.
Their lips touch like the lips of lovers.
Then they disappear—plus one
and minus one cancelling themselves out.
No drumrolls or flashes of light, no screams.
Such is the joy of self gorging on self,
leaving in its wake only the smallest of sounds,
a single wrinkle in the smooth fabric of the night:
something like a hiccup, something like a sob.

EYELIDS

Shy defiers of the existential world,
you draw your veil across the unpleasant,
then the head turns away, the body turns away,
the feet trudge off toward someplace nice, but you,
you were the first, you drew the initial curtain.

Oh, cautious celebrators of the decorous,
how much has gone unwitnessed or unjudged,
how much remains unchanged due to your benign
interference? Why reduce the world to this
middle range of behavior, as if the story

contained only happy couples on lawn chairs
nibbling macaroons and sipping soothing drinks.
Don't you fear the darkness will squeeze you tight
because of your ignorance of it?
Oh, my shy ones, forgive this desecration—

the chrome of the scissors will sparkle in your eyes,
while your being closed only simplifies my task.
A few quick snips and the light will shine forever.
Gaze upon it. See that fire, those cold stones.
This is the world to love. There is no other.

DESIRE

A woman in my class wrote that she is sick
of men wanting her body and when she reads
her poem out loud the other women all nod
and even some of the men lower their eyes

and look abashed as if ready to unscrew
their cocks and pound down their own dumb heads
with these innocent sausages of flesh, and none
would think of confessing his hunger

or admit how desire can ring like a constant
low note in the brain or grant how the sight
of a beautiful woman can make him groan
on those first spring days when the parkas

have been packed away and the bodies are staring
at the bodies and the eyes stare at the ground;
and there was a man I knew who even at ninety
swore that his desire had never diminished.

Is this simply the wish to procreate, the world
telling the cock to eat faster, while the cock
yearns for that moment when it forgets its loneliness
and the world flares up in an explosion of light?

Why have men been taught to feel ashamed
of their desire, as if each were a criminal
out on parole, a desperado with a long record
of muggings, rapes, such conduct as excludes

*   *   *

each one from all but the worst company,
and never to be trusted, no never to be trusted?
Why must men pretend to be indifferent as if each
were a happy eunuch engaged in spiritual thoughts?

But it's the glances that I like, the quick ones,
the unguarded ones, like a hand snatching a pie
from a window ledge and the feet pounding away;
eyes fastening on a leg, a breast, the curve

of a buttock, as the pulse takes an extra thunk
and the cock, that toothless worm, stirs in its sleep,
and fat possibility swaggers into the world
like a big spender entering a bar. And sometimes

the woman glances back. Oh, to disappear
in a tangle of fabric and flesh as the cock
sniffs out its little cave, and the body hungers
for closure, for the completion of the circle,

as if each of us were born only half a body
and we spend our lives searching for the rest.
What good does it do to deny desire, to chain
the cock to the leg and scrawl a black **X**

across its bald head, to hold out a hand
for each passing woman to slap? Better
to be bad and unrepentant, better to celebrate
each difference, not to be cruel or gluttonous

*   *   *

or over-bearing, but full of hope and self-forgiving.
The flesh yearns to converse with other flesh.
Each pore loves to linger over its particular story.
Let these seconds not be full of self-recrimination

and apology. What is desire but the wish for some
relief from the self, the prisoner let out
into a small square of sunlight with a single
red flower and a bird crossing the sky, to lean back

against the bricks with the legs outstretched,
to feel the sun warming the brow, before returning
to one's mortal cage, steel doors slamming
in the cell block, steel bolts sliding shut?

ROOTLESS

He must have been born with greased feet
to keep sliding so, born at the pinnacle
of a glass hill and then released,

a life spent in the articulation
of hellos and goodbyes. How many times
has he carried boxes through doorways?

The key turns in the ignition, the view
in the rearview mirror repeats itself
and once more his tires caress the road,

their only love. He had hoped to stop this.
He had thought that by buying things
he could hang possessions from his body

like sandbags from a balloon. He had thought
that by acquiring a wife and family
he was at last planting himself, his two feet

sunk knee deep in concrete, but anything
can be packed and his children's heads
peak cunningly from their cartons.

At best he can slow the rate of departure,
not move faster and faster, to take pleasure
in the experienced moment, not the next one,

the potential one. Still, he has often seen,
when returning to visit some place he had
left some years before, the same people

*   *   *

sitting at the same tables in the same cafés,
the same jokes, same love affairs, the same
houses being painted over and over, lives

fixed like stones along a stream, watching
the water chortle by, the same weather,
even the same birds twittering overhead.

Better fashion from his life a boat
with nothing to catch him but time itself,
that distant cataract. Better take with him

only those few possessions he values—
the wing of a sparrow to remind him
of his loyalties, a blue glass marble

to teach him the folly of standing still
and a box of air, pure air, to show him
where he has come from and what lies ahead.

FOLK TALES

Sometimes looking over your shoulder
into the past you have such a sense
of all those things better left undone—
the anger you shouldn't have expressed,
the words better left unspoken,
the woman it was wrong to kiss—
that looking back is like looking back
on breakage, a tangle of wrong turns,
a morass of the inappropriate and inopportune;
that what exists back there is such a wreckage
it seems astonishing you have ever reached
any place at all, that the one vehicle
you haven't smashed against a wall
is time itself, that time has put you here
as much as gravity drops a boulder
from a cliff face to the road below
where it might crush a car or might not.
But it isn't time or gravity
that is responsible, you are responsible,
you are always responsible. But then
looking into the future, sifting through
all those plans and good intentions,
you know full well that in ten years
you will still be looking back and still
finding breakage, until you want to turn
to the people around you, turn even
to strangers and say, I'm sorry, I'm sorry;
so that some days you raise a foot
and the foot seems so heavy and the step
so long that you think why bother,

and you hang there a moment
like a marionette with tangled strings,
until you heave your foot forward, a creature
in a story maybe two thirds over.
You think of those folk tales where two brothers
are sent out on two separate journeys
and one meets with great good fortune
and the other disaster, while both
at any given time are full of hope
and bragging to themselves, At last
I've got it right, and see their road
as the lucky one, while the question
of how this story will reach its conclusion
becomes the one reason you keep reading
late, late into the night, as your wife
with her beautiful body sleeps alone
in the next room, and your children
lie unkissed in their beds, and all through
the city the lights are blinking out.

SUMMER EVENINGS

As I finish my wine, I think of my friends.
Right now each is doing some particular thing,
sleeping or making love or reading a book.
Here it is autumn. A car in the street
keeps honking its horn, then roars away,

squealing its tires. When we were last together
it was in the country. The sun had set
and in the room where we sat a single lamp
was burning, its red shade casting a glow.
Two were reading, others were talking.

A moth kept flinging itself at the light,
batting its wings on the shade, till someone
caught it and took it outside. I wanted
to touch these people, explain how much
they meant to me and how my life felt

enriched by them. Briefly, the moment hung
like a single drop of water from a faucet,
and the very second felt split open: a rock
in which one finds a tiny cave filled
with bright crystals. But then a car began

honking from someplace nearby, an angry
jittery noise, and when at last it stopped,
the drop had fallen and had begun its journey,
the solitary journey made by each of us,
rushing streams, broad rivers, unknown seas.

CAREERS

How difficult it was to look at them
and how hard it has been to come to the memory—
a room crowded with elderly nuns on the top floor
of a hospital in Kalamazoo more than twenty years ago.
I was still in graduate school and taking a break
to earn money and write, and I recall
writing a poem about Ulysses coming back
and another about a quest. How simple it seemed
to pick a life and have that life make sense.
That was what was easy about being twenty-four.
So it felt correct to choose what seemed hardest,
where the spiritual return was greatest.
That year I worked at a Catholic college
and my closest friend was a nun of about eighty
plagued by bad feet, which was why she'd been sent
to the hospital. At that time the nuns still wore
the full habit, black of course, with only
their hands and faces uncovered and a great
silver cross around their necks. One never saw
their hair or any trace of their bodies, everything
was concealed in the service of their calling,
and I was struck by their wedding rings—these brides
of Christ. Clearly, I was nervous about visiting
my friend, of seeing a whole floor of sick nuns,
afraid of seeing one undressed or somehow revealed,
so it was at least a week before I finally went.
I was also writing a novel and had constant plans,
a whole career under way, and the next year back
in graduate school I even wrote a poem about this visit,
although I didn't get it right or really know
what it meant, had only been amazed, even shocked,

when I had walked down the hall and then stopped
to look through the doorway of a ward—twenty or
twenty-five women in their eighties and nineties
propped up in chairs and couches, their habits askew,
their wimples twisted to reveal a hank of hair,
stick figures lost within yards of black cloth.
But more striking than the nuns were the dolls
that at least a dozen held—rocking and soothing them,
patting their backs, clucking and cooing to them.
One singing in a cracked voice, another clutching
the doll to her bony shoulder. How much love they had
for these rag things as they stroked and caressed them
and I remember one nun by the door with her face
scrunched into a thousand wrinkles as she aped
the doting expression of a young mother. And then
came my shock at the dolls themselves:
colorless and faceless, with their features
rubbed off, stroked, kissed off, until from
top to bottom they had turned uniformly gray,
some yarn for the hair, nothing for the eyes,
handed on from one elderly nun to another,
a comfort in their last years, before death plucked
those childless women from their chosen calling.

SKELETON

That human pyramid those circus
gymnasts build—fifteen men,
while the one on top, five layers up,
blows kisses to the crowd: can it dance?

Step by painful step it staggers
undaunted across the ring. Likewise
the skeleton is such an accumulation
of bone piled on bone, hung all about

with muscles, organs, tissue, blood,
while the skin—a great rubbery bag—
keeps the bits all bunched together:
sometimes it's pretty, sometimes it barely

gets by. But within it plod and sweat
those gymnasts, daredevils perched
on each other's shoulders, while the clown
on top corkscrews his whole carcass

into an effortless smile. Escaped
dog dinners, Halloween phantasm—
the skeleton grunts through its day
weighed down by all the body, as if

the fifteen men had to balance baskets
of luncheon meats, trunks of clothes,
two skittish goats, several sets
of socket wrenches and a hat rack.

*　　*　　*

Shouldn't we applaud how it drops nothing,
how it plods step by impossible step,
not graceful, but full of courage;
no genius, but immensely stubborn?

But the crowd drifts off elsewhere:
couples on first dates begin to smooch,
kids suck their soft drinks and a blonde
in a feathered boa powders her nose.

Outside the tent the wild animal tamer
leans against a wagon and smokes a cheroot.
Just how many stars are there up there?
he thinks. What's behind the black space?

Through the tent flap he sees the gymnasts
finish their act to tired applause. They are
for him a performer's performer and allow
the crowd to think this marvel of endurance

is just a joke, which soothes them, gives
the rubes a breather, before the animal act
cranks up and the lions, like a whiff of ruin,
dismember the complacency with their roars.

THE BODY'S CURSE

Sad to say there's more than one—loneliness
for example. What a devil. No one understands you,
no one wants to touch you, while the skin grows cold
and the mind has all the vigor of wet paper.

Yet I know people who are so distrustful
of the folks around them that when anyone gets
too close, they push them away. Get lost, they say.
Of course they are miserable, the poor babies,

but they think it is better to be tough from the start,
than to have some trickster turn on them later.
Loneliness for them is what's safest, although
no one is happy or likes getting up in the morning,

no one sings in the shower. And then there's pride:
that sense of self that says the self's first rate.
But how hungry it gets, how malnourished, and how
it poisons the world. I knew a fellow who received

a great gift and because someone he despised
was given an equal gift he destroyed his own.
His pride made each thing smaller than it was,
leaving him bitter, dissatisfied. And then

we have opinions, those conclusions which say
that what you don't know don't count: the ballot box
is closed, the votes are tallied and the decision
is reached that the world is flat or she loves you

*   *   *

not or that man's a fool. So even the smartest
grow ignorant and stumble through the twilight
like all the rest. And then ambition, that quest
to leave the road behind one packed with monuments

to one's own perfection, a statue in the park
to show the world one isn't the jerk one thinks
in those dark moments of the night. Or sexual hunger,
thirsting for ladies as a bowling ball thirsts for pins,

then casting them aside, the beauty forgotten
while still clasped in a post-orgasmic embrace.
Greed, gluttony, sloth—but don't they all
go back to loneliness, that sense of a barrier

between oneself and others, as if they see differently,
feel differently, as if one were a dog surrounded
by skeptical cats? And so a man develops pride,
ambition and all the rest, just to prove

that the awful place with which he has been blessed
is a blessing after all. He may *seem* miserable—
the loneliness gnawing him like a cancer—
but actually that pain is the pain of success,

and he makes his little smile that creaks
and walks on, while what he really wants
is to be held and stroked and be told: Poor thing.
Yet even were he to get it he would break it,

*   *   *

like someone giving him a ceramic plate,
he would hurl it to the sidewalk, hitch up
his pants and hobble away. What can be done?
Who can say what another man wants?

Ask the mouth, it says More. Ask the feet,
they say Faster. Try the hands, they say Mine.
Question the whole crazy and quarrelsome
conglomeration, and it says Touch me.

CEZANNE AND ZOLA

At thirteen they were known as the inseparables.
"Opposites by nature," wrote Zola, "we became
united forever in the midst of the brutal gang
of dreadful dunces who beat us." Inconsolable
with Zola in Paris, Cézanne wrote, "I no longer
recognize myself. I am heavy, stupid and slow."
Despite many visits, their disagreements overthrew
their intimacy and they grew apart. "A dreamer,"
was how Zola described his friend, "a failure
of genius." And in a novel he wrote how Cézanne
"had lost his footing and drowned in the dazzling
folly of art." Cézanne replied with sixteen years
of silence, yet when Zola died he fled to his room.
"All day," a friend said, "we heard the sound of weeping."

CEZANNE'S SUCCESS

The girls he followed down the street, the heartbreaks
he pretended to suffer, the giddy letters he wrote
to Zola with pages of bad poetry, bad jokes
to conceal his fear of being dull, the self-doubts
he laughed about, the shyness overcome by wine,
this world began to collapse when he undertook
his own inflexible path, his discipline
leading him further into isolation. "Whoever lacks
a taste for the absolute, meaning perfection,"
he wrote, "contents himself with mediocrity."
His misfortune was his own determined study:
"Art is a religion. Its aim is the elevation
of mind." No jokes, no girls, no wine. The friends
stopped calling. Harsh wind at night, no loving hands.

CEZANNE'S OUTRAGEOUSNESS

"Like a child," Mary Cassatt said, describing
how Cézanne resembled a cutthroat, but seemed gentle,
and that he ate scraping his soup plate, pouring
the last drops into his spoon, was deferential
to the stupid maid, held his chop in one hand,
ripping the meat with his teeth, clutched his knife
in his clenched fist the entire meal, a kind
of baton to accompany each word, each loud laugh.
"Appearances cannot be relied on over here,"
she wrote, impressed, but thinking him outrageous.
"Isolation is all I'm good for," he said in a letter,
"then at least no one gets me in his clutches."
While another painter quoted him to prove him mad:
"I am the only one alive who can paint a red."

ADAM

It was something like a hole in the air,
a blank place in the Garden. All else
he had studied—each animal, each flower,
to everything else he had given a name—

only this tree with its peculiar fruit,
which, by being nameless, became most visible,
the bruise one is trying to ignore, while
in its presence a whole body disappears.

It was wrong to blame the woman.
Probably she didn't say no loudly enough,
no more than that. Probably she only said
it was a bad idea or you'd better not.

And he shook his head and turned away.
One never hears how long he held out—
a month, a year, ten years. How long
did it keep sticking its pin in him,

this fictitious vacancy? Until, of course,
he had to name it, taste it, touch each leaf.
What were his regrets after the expulsion?
At least nothing was left to surprise him.

And whatever he named that fruit he probably
called it most bountiful, because it taught him
the very worst, and wouldn't this protect him,
wouldn't it be a weapon against all to come?

LONG STORY

There must have been a moment after the expulsion
from the Garden when the animals were considering
what to do next and just who was in charge.
The bear flexed his muscles, the tiger flashed
his claws, and even the porcupine thought himself
fit to rule and showed off the knife points
of his quills. No one noticed the hairless creatures,
with neither sharp teeth, nor talons, they were too puny.
It was then Cain turned and slew his own brother
and Abel's white body lay sprawled in the black dirt
as if it had already lain cast down forever.
What followed was an instant of prophetic thought
as the trees resettled themselves, the grass
dug itself deeper into the ground and all
grew impressed by the hugeness of Cain's desire.
He must really want to be boss, said the cat.
This was the moment when the animals surrendered
the power of speech as they crept home to the bosoms
of their families, the prickly ones, the smelly ones,
the ones they hoped would never do them harm.
Who could envy Cain his hunger? Better to be circumspect
and silent. Better not to want the world too much.
Left alone with the body of his brother, Cain began
to assemble the words about what Abel had done
and what he had been forced to do in return.
It was a long story. It took his entire life
to tell it. And even then it wasn't finished.
How great language had to become to encompass
its deft evasions and sly contradictions,
its preenings and self-satisfied gloatings.

Each generation makes a contribution, hoping
to have got it right at last. The sun rises
and sets. The leaves flutter like a million
frightened hands. Confidently, we step forward
and tack a few meager phrases onto the end.

THE PROOF

The body's fear is to be forcibly overthrown
and so it sets out this fence of pain
to warn it when the world has crept too close.
The intruder intrudes, the skin shrieks
and the body hastens away. This barrier

gives us our identity, marking off
the territory of the self, like seeing
different farmers' fields from a plane:
those multicolored shapes each with fences
set in between. What would happen otherwise?

Would we blend with the sky, become
like cloud or smoke, or would we merge
with each other? This woman that I love,
if we felt no pain would I so force myself
upon her that we would join together

like two plucked chickens in a plastic bag?
Is it just pain that keeps us separate,
that forms the frontier of our loneliness
and without it we would all jumble together
into one bright color? But the body insists

on being individual and erects its barriers
which protect it even from its desires,
since one can be defeated from within
as well as from without; and I remember
a child I knew at a camp, a boy about ten,

*   *   *

who had been born without a sense of pain
and who had gnawed off half his fingers,
bitten pieces from his arms, now covered
with bandages, and how we had to spy on him
just to protect him from this private feast.

I would check his cabin late at night,
flick on my flashlight and find him wide awake,
his face caught in the circle of light,
his own flesh in his mouth, chewing, chewing,
as if he meant to pass his whole being

across his tongue. The coils of barbed wire
surrounding his body were gone and he was
slipping away. What secret place did he hope
to reach through the doorway of his mouth?
Or was that place simply his own life?

Our sense of touch limits and defines us.
Without it this boy was a shadow, a dream
of his own imagination. How else could he survive?
Pain corroborates the world. His body's
taste between his teeth proved he was alive.

FREIGHT CARS

Once, taking a train into Chicago
from the west, I saw a message
scrawled on a wall in the railway yard—
Tommy, call home, we need you—
and for years I have worried, imagining
the worst scenarios. Beneath the message
was a number written in red chalk,
although at eighteen who was I to call
and at forty-six who is left to listen?
But Tommy, I think of him still traveling
out in the country, riding freight car
after freight car, just squeaking by
in pursuit of some private quest.
That's the problem, isn't it?
Coming into the world and imagining
some destination for oneself,
some place to make all the rest
all right, as we cast aside those
who love us, as they cast aside others
in their turn, and all of us
wandering, wandering in a direction
which only our vanity claims to be forward,
while the messages fall away like pathetic cries—
come back, call home, we need you.

BRINK

My son stands at the shore's lip
and skips flat stones across the water.
He carries a wooden sword in his belt
which occasionally he pulls out
and ponders, before returning to skipping stones.
He is ready for any adventure
and waits on the brink like someone
waiting in line. Soon the show will start,
soon it will be his turn. What
would knowledge give him but fear?
Around him the birds are pursuing their dinners,
the bugs, while the bugs are pursuing their dinners,
the smaller bugs. The old image comes like a vision—
the blind boy on the cliff playing his flute.
How he dances and kicks up his feet
above the chasm. Wasn't this always the case?
And won't the story be repeated until we ourselves
take the page and tear it from the book?

SHRILL

Like an abandoned car, engine gone,
tires missing, or like a bag of trash left
at the curb which the dogs have torn open
so this woman had become scattered, broken,
and she slept in bus stations and alleys,
a thin dark woman in her thirties
with a smell like a swamp; but her tongue
grew sharper than ever as she spat her scorn
at police, social workers, shop keepers,
to all who spoke, whether to help or hurt her,
to all she would voice the stink of the world,
the stink of being alive; so that even her body
became a voice, a strident voice with its
rags and dirt and the tangled filth of her hair
and wherever she went whether around
Boston or Harvard Square she became a shrill
retribution, an attack on the eye, a judgment
against those hearty buyers and spenders—
the stink of the world, stink of being alive—
until each person was cloaked with the coarse dust
of her abuse, until the sky seemed gray with it
and the city echoed it, until one day somebody
could no longer stand it and trapped her
in the lobby of a building in Brookline
and stuck a knife in her over and over,
somebody for whom her voice had become
a torture destroyed her and escaped unnoticed:
so one last time the police phoned her brother,
a writer, and her father, a rabbi—kind people
for whom her cry goes on undiminished.

HOW COULD YOU EVER BE FINE?

For S.C.

I dreamt last night I heard someone speak your name,
two women were talking about you and I went to them
and asked about you and they gave me your number.
So I called you and we talked and you said
you were fine, and I doubted it was really you,
because how could you ever be fine? What have
twenty years done to you? Where are you now?
You had the smoothest skin, a face like a beautiful
wax figure as you moved from one messed up man
to another. There was one who used to shoot up
Jack Daniels, and when I told him that was stupid,
he said, That's right, I'm stupid, I'm really stupid,
somebody should kill me! Until I said it actually
wasn't so stupid just to calm him. But all those men
who hit you and abused you and how you explained
they must have been right or else they wouldn't
have done it. I was too tame, didn't stick myself
with pins or know the names for all the drugs,
and had a vague idea of what I wanted to do
next week, next year. You would listen with one
black eye swollen half shut, then go back to the guy
who had done it so he could blacken the other.
I remember you told me how your mother had said
it was your duty to love her, and you shouted, No,
and kept shouting no. And when she died you felt glad,
but years later I took you to one funeral director
after another so you could find her ashes.
You said you wanted to talk to her, a beautiful
woman telling her troubles to a cardboard box.

Then you would sprinkle her ashes into the canal
and feel something, you weren't sure what, maybe
just done with something, the sense that something
was over. But either we couldn't find the right
funeral director or the ashes were already gone,
and that night you went back to a man who beat you,
and shortly after that you slipped out of my life—
a few cards, a few phone calls, then nothing.
Right now you are either out there or you're not—
smoking a cigarette, touching a sore place, looking
from the window and letting all the old faces
drift across your mind. It is hard to think of you
dowdy and forty, the problems dealt with, a life
of some sort on track, hard to think of you making it
past twenty-five. At least in books we know the end,
know the characters died or got married, had great
success or failure. But you are out there someplace,
and your friend who shot up the Jack Daniels,
and the guy I took the knife away from,
and the other who wanted to be a writer,
and the girl who quit school to have a baby,
and another girl who smashed the doors of my truck
on an acid trip. They are all out there, just
putting one foot in front of another, just like
the torturers are out there, and the men who worked
on firing squads, and the men who like to hit things
just to hurt them. And you are out there too,
picking your way between the paper, the tin cans,
the broken glass. You had the most wonderful smile.
On whom does it shine now, whom does it welcome?
People on hard streets dragged to inevitable ends.

HOW YOU ARE LINKED

There are days when you wake and your body
feels too long or too short, like a shirt
shrunk in the wash, or a fisherman's net
that has somehow ensnared you, and it feels

as if your body were swapped in the night
for the body of a stranger, and your whole day
is spent searching. Whose body am I wearing,
where has my old self gone off to? If it is winter,

then it is raining. If summer, then the day
is thick with humidity and hot, and fat
clouds jerk across the sky like stupid thoughts.
These are the days when closets are searched,

when you find yourself standing in a corner
of the cellar not knowing how you got there,
when your body keeps slipping from your shoulders
or gripping you too tightly around the neck;

when you yell at your wife without reason
and your children avoid you and the dog hides
under a bush. But then sometimes it happens
that late in the afternoon, you decide

that the body you are wearing belongs to someone
you knew as a child, a kid up the street
or a girl with braces or a third grade boy
who was never popular and whom you teased

*   *   *

with the rest, putting a dead frog in his desk
or pinning a kick me sign to the collar
of his shirt, but now he is grown up and maybe
he works for a bank or is a radio engineer

but he still has two left feet and a hesitant
way of talking and somehow in the night
you have gotten his body, even though
you haven't seen him for thirty years or know

whether he lives in Detroit or Schenectady,
but it must be him because you recognize
the way he hunched his shoulders and kept
his body clenched, and you recall how once

you stood by as the class bully baited him
into tears while you shuffled your feet
and did nothing, or when you discovered
he liked some girl, you mocked her shyness

or fatness or dumbness until he was forced
to ridicule her just to keep some scrap
of self-respect, and now you are stuck
in his body and it feels like a discarded

high school locker that you have gotten yourself
crammed into with snapped-off hooks and rusty
hinges and a defective combination lock
and you can't seem to get out or know how

*   *   *

to get back to yourself again or why
you ever treated this boy so badly with his
funny walk or legs which must have been
too tight just as they are too tight for you.

Such is your mental tumult and tangle
that you drag through the day unable to speak
to your wife or daughters who don't know why
you are acting so strangely, who don't realize

you are trapped in the adult body of a boy
you abused so long ago. But perhaps because he
crowds your thoughts, that night you dream of him
and he doesn't look too peculiar even though

his red hair still sticks up in back. Is he
wearing your body? You can't be sure, but yes
it suits him pretty well and he moves it
confidently and without discomfort. How

is his life different from yours? He tells you
of an adequate job, of a family who loves him,
and you begin to think how good he looks,
how in fact your lives are almost identical:

two men with the same neckties, same chitchat,
same shaggy dogs; and even though you don't
discuss the past somehow an understanding
is reached, words of affection are exchanged,

*   *   *

and after promising to write he fades off
into the confusion that borders all your dreams.
When you wake in the morning, you touch yourself
all over. This bag of flesh, is it yours or his?

Then you recognize a mole, a scar and soon
you conclude that your old body is your burden
once again. Joyfully, you leap from bed.
But isn't this the moment when you should stop

and recollect, when you should write yourself
a little note just so you won't forget how it felt
to be lost in another man's body, how entangled
it got, how claustrophobic and how guilty

you felt? But of course you don't because
you are too excited and the sky is welcoming
and the streets are full of people to be touched,
and you rush off to the old patterns, old mistakes,

your own personal combination of running
and falling, as you grow ever more separate,
more isolated, pursuing your path like a crook
alone in a bank vault, until again the world

must remind you of how you are linked, grabbing
your lapels and smacking your face, hurling you
into a stranger's body. Who's this? you say,
as if it were some stray beauty, the seduced

*   *   *

victim of late night desire. But hidden within
this newcomer lurks only yourself: the monster,
the treasure, the curiosity you have passionately
tried to decipher for all the years of your life.

SPLEEN

Oh, much maligned one, meager hunkerer
beneath the heart, they slander you
who claim that anger is your little engine,
that melancholy squats within you
like a frog in its rank grotto. My hands
feel anger, my fingers feel anger, but you
in your basement chamber, you doze to the steady
whoosh of my lungs, diminutive carwash
of the blood, extracting a few dead cells
like a monkey picking lice from its mate,
but nothing serious, nothing professional
like the liver—for you it is simply a hobby.
I knew a doctor once who had a bookcase full
of your brothers and sisters preserved in bottles
while their former hosts still strolled the streets.
I asked, Do those people persist
in feeling anger? Do they ever grow sad?
He thought I was crazy and drove me away.
But a friend with a missing spleen still
fights and rages in shoddy bars or stares out
at the moon racing behind clouds and weeps.

Little tousler of tired erythrocytes,
do they mean to say that without you
my love of life would flow unchecked,
a constant good humor untainted
by proof of falsehood, injustice or greed?
If true, then bankers would have made sure
centuries ago that each child's spleen
would be plucked out at birth, and the courts
would have declared you a common criminal,

known for your tangle of mood changes
concerning unlimited buying and spending.
No, my pygmy pacifist, my anger is my own.
It is the sweetener I use to taste the world.
It trickles from my body like sweat.
How could my love be so great if that love
throbbed unqualified? Return to sleep,
oh superfluous one, and we'll stand sentry
above your uselessness—I with my doubting,
my anger with its club, and melancholy
with its constant image of a double world:
the one, our burden, and the other, our dream.

THE BODY'S HOPE

Whatever lifts the body up—muscles,
sinews, joints; whatever wrestles against
gravity itself—the raised step, the lifted arm—
these form the body's hope. But also hunger,

selfishness, desire, all that leads us
to put one foot in front of the other,
these too form the body's hope, whatever
combats that urge to lie down—greed,

anger, lust—these feelings keep us going,
while the imagination sketches pictures
of the desired future, how we will look
in that new hat, how we will feel

with a belly full of cherries: anything
that shoves us from this moment to the next,
motivation like a flight of stairs, and hope
like a push at the top, not dissatisfaction

but eagerness to plunge into the next second:
hope like a policeman urging the crowd along,
the travel agent with enticing descriptions
of where to go next, the tour guide director

with someplace specific to get to before dark.
You know those French chateaux where you stop
for a few hours on a summer afternoon,
how you are ushered through the ornate front doors,

*   *   *

shown the bed where Louis the Something slept,
the chair where Madame de Maintenon sat,
then you are shown through a door in the back,
and it is over and the peacocks cry their

abrasive cries and you return to your cars?
Life struggles to copy that French chateau,
while the hope is the person leading you through
with promises of the splendor of the next room.

But the great bed looks fusty and hard,
and the chair is just a chair and on the way out
you pass tourists coming in and you want to tell them
not to bother, but hope has you by the arm.

Without hope we'd still be learning how to crawl,
while thinking, What's the point? We'd still
be staring into our first bowl of porridge
and fiddling with our spoons. Hope moves our feet.

It is the constant encourager, the enemy
of the stationary, the promiser of better moments.
In the next room waits a woman to curl our toes,
then a twelve pound diamond, then the prize

to raise us higher than all the rest—oh, why
aren't we running faster?—hope: our dearest
enemy, slick-talking advance man for death itself,
and the back door beckons and the peacocks cry.

CEZANNE'S COLDNESS

Another person's hand upon his arm, the threat
of an embrace, the bumping together of people in crowds,
strange flesh against his flesh, such episodes
would leave him in a huff. "My father hates
to be touched," his son would say. Who could guess
his shyness or know how the unexpected touch
could overthrow his self-control and breech
his defenses with the hope of intimacy?
A hope he saw as false, and so he raged.
It wasn't too little emotion but too much
that caused him to seem cold. He despised how a touch
could make him yearn for more, and so he salvaged
some scrap of self with anger. Better to loathe them.
Better to spit or they'd stick their hooks in him.

CEZANNE'S ANGER

Around the building where he worked, a tangle
of jungle, bushes and shrubs pressed close
to the walls of yellow concrete as if to strangle
this high-ceilinged second floor room whose
tall windows rose above the trees, a bare-walled,
light-filled room with pottery, wax fruit,
some poetry, four human skulls. Outside it all
a gate and stone wall shielding it from the street.
His courtesy was like that wall, a mild façade
behind which his rage swirled uncontrolled, a frenzy
surrounding the cool place where he worked, ready
to destroy any painting which he felt had failed,
when he yanked open his windows and flung the ugly,
the slack or stupid canvas into the ravenous trees.

CEZANNE'S PORTRAITS

In Cézanne's portraits of his family it seems
that either they disliked him or he disliked them
or he chose to paint them as if they disliked him—
the father reading, the wife holding her anger in,
the son, Paul, expecting to be yelled at, looking
somewhat foolish with his moony face, derby hat—
"my horizon," his father called him, yet whose fate
was to squander a fortune at cards and gambling.
Another portrait shows Paul lying on the grass,
staring into the distance. This time his wariness
is softened by the summer day and running brook:
a wistful expression his father knew and undertook
to put down exactly, because wasn't it also his own:
the desire to escape his enemies, to be alone?

THOUGHTS AT THIRTY
THOUSAND FEET

The penny holds out its little promise:
Why boredom? Why bread? Why cereal
without sugar? And so the child discovers
discontent. Who of us can now remember

what we were doing when we first understood
the concept of More? Possibly the child was
sniffing at flowers, or fixing the paw
of a sick puppy, or plunk-plunking his heart out

on a toy piano, when, as if from far away,
came the gentle persuasion of nickle plinking
against nickle, and the child lifted his head
and perked up his ears. Is there any doubt

why he takes that first step? But how sturdy
and persistent are the ears, the one part
of the body to keep growing, when all the rest
stops. Clearly, they fatten with our desire

as we hurry after each possible new offer.
Consider the oversized ears of the elderly,
like the cross section of a boiled red pepper,
as they strain to hear the seductions of lucre.

I think of this tonight on the plane, surrounded
by my brothers, the soldiers of the dollar,
who sit at rest, their short leashes dangling
free at their necks, the paraphernalia

           *   *   *

of counting all stowed away, and their ears,
their sad unlovely ears at last at peace.
Perhaps they will fold up like flowers, close
like the bright faces of sunflowers

till the new day beckons and once more
they pursue their god's triumphant march
across the sky. It seems unlikely. Even
in deepest sleep the ears hear the voices

of their tempters whispering More and Not Enough.
Even dead they keep listening and expanding,
filling their graves as love fills the heart,
and only that fat stone with their names

and dates and those lies about how much
they are missed—only that stone pressing
like a locked door against the earth
to keep the whole mess from exploding.

WHAT YOU SHOULD HAVE THOUGHT ABOUT EARLIER

Twelve murderers are eating their dinners,
veal cutlet and walnuts, pickled pigs' feet.
Somebody sticks his head through the door.
The inevitable question is asked.
Not me, says Biter; nor me, says Shooter.
We didn't do it, say Choker and Stabber.
Nor me, nor me, say all the others.
The door closes with a bang.
The bad chaps return to their meal,
just shoveling the food with both hands,
slurping their jaws as they chew,
swallowing with great gulps, then belching,
picking their teeth with their daggers. Afterward
they stagger toward the door and lurch down
the street. Back to work, they happily shout.

And you, shopping or walking or simply standing still,
you better lift up your feet and trot home,
bolt those deadbolt locks, crawl under the covers.
Your brothers and sisters are coming to get you,
the ones you had forgotten about,
the ones you should have thought about earlier.
Ring ding goes the doorbell. Welcome to crazy times.

CONFESSION

The Nazi within me thinks it's time to take charge.
The world's a mess; people are crazy.
The Nazi within me wants windows shut tight,
new locks put on the doors. There's too much
fresh air, too much coming and going.
The Nazi within me wants more respect. He wants
the only TV camera, the only bank account,
the only really pretty girl. The Nazi within me
wants to be boss of traffic and traffic lights.
People drive too fast; they take up too much space.
The Nazi within me thinks people are getting away
with murder. He wants to be boss of murder.
He wants to be boss of bananas, boss of white bread.
The Nazi within me wants uniforms for everyone.
He wants them to wash their hands, sit up straight,
pay strict attention. He wants to make certain
they say yes when he says yes, no when he says no.
He imagines everybody sitting in straight chairs,
people all over the world sitting in straight chairs.
Are you ready? he asks them. They say they are ready.
Are you ready to be happy? he asks them. They say
they are ready to be happy. The Nazi within me wants
everyone to be happy but not too happy and definitely
not noisy. No singing, no dancing, no carrying on.

NO MAP

How close the clouds press this October first
and the rain—a gray scarf across the sky.
In separate hospitals my father and a dear friend
lie waiting for their respective operations,
hours on a table as surgeons crack their chests.
They were so brave when I talked to them last
as they spoke of the good times we would share
in the future. To neither did I say how much
I loved them, nor express the extent of my fear.
Their bodies are delicate glass boxes
at which the world begins to fling its stones.
Is this the day their long cry will be released?
How can I live in this place without them?
But today is also my son's birthday.
He is eight and beginning his difficult march.
To him the sky is welcoming, the road straight.
Far from my house he will open his presents—
a book, a Swiss army knife, some music. Where
is his manual of instructions? Where is his map
showing the dark places and how to escape them?

IN A ROW

The mailman handing me a letter,
he paid a little. My daughter's

third grade teacher, the electrician
putting a light over my back door:

they paid as well. The woman at the bank
who cashes my check. She paid a part of it.

The typist in my office, the janitor
sweeping the floor—they paid some too.

The movie star paid for it. The nurse,
the nun, the saint, they all paid for it—

a photograph from Central America,
six children lying neatly in a row.

One day I was teaching or I sold
a book review or I gave a lecture

and some of the money came to me
and some rolled off into the world,

but it was still my money, the result
of my labor, each coin still had my name

printed across it, and I went on living,
passing my days in a box with a tight lid.

*   *   *

But elsewhere, skulking through tall grass,
a dozen men approached a village. It was hot;

the men made no noise. See that one's cap,
see the button on that other man's shirt,

hear the click of the cartridge as it slides
into its chamber, see the handkerchief

which that man uses to wipe his brow—
I paid for that one, that one belongs to me.

CANTO HONDO

For three days the goat was tied to the stoop,
a cabrito, the two Antonios called it,
a small gray goat running skittishly across
the white steps, or shying away as we passed,

my wife and I and the baby in the backpack;
and the Antonios would point to the goat
and grin, and speak again about the weekend
when the goat would be cooked in the fireplace

with potatoes and olive oil and garlic—
the younger Antonio an electrician and alcoholic,
resembling a small Humphrey Bogart; the older,
his cousin, also alcoholic and the owner

of a bodega in this village in Granada province
grown rich from cherimoyas, so that one found
dozens of bodegas and alcoholics and everyone
was related, so that all day came the sound of

Primo, primo, cousin, cousin, and the invitation
to have a little drink. My friend was living
with the younger Antonio and we were visiting,
a marriage as shaky as a skiff in rough water

with the baby a kind of anchor, but the party
would be a time out period and the postman
would sing canto hondo, and Maria, half-paralyzed
and three hundred pounds, owner of her own bodega,

*   *   *

53

would sing in her child's voice, and the beautician
would dance and the two Antonios would hammer
their spoons on the table top all in honor
of the Americans with their shaky marriage.

Why did I pass those days in suspicion,
wondering what task would be asked of me next?
I would watch the goat with a perverse
identification, and imagine rescuing it,

taking it back to the States, until the goat
became the outward shape of all my discontent,
until its pathetic bleats became my own whinings,
until its tuggings and various dartings became

my own desire to escape, until the older Antonio
simply killed it in a great slaughter as the goat
fought and actually kicked out his two front teeth
before Antonio cut its throat on the top step,

letting its blood splash over the rest, so that
for days we would tramp over this palpable memory
of the party, first red, then brown, until the rain
washed off all but a few stubborn stains.

But Antonio, what joy he took in pointing
to his mouth and shattered teeth; and I mistakenly
thought he was crazy or drunk, because how happily
he kept saying that now he would never forget,

* * *

that ten times a day he would recall the goat
and the American couple with el rubio
in the backpack, and he would point to his mouth
and claim how lucky he was that this great

occasion would be with him always, while I
could hardly twist my mouth into a smile,
seeing it as an ordeal to be slogged through,
keeping myself clenched, completely confusing

Antonio's pleasure at his splintered teeth,
that he had found a way to box a series of events
while he sang and ate the cabrito, which he was
sharing with his good friends, an occasion

he would re-experience each time he glanced
in the mirror, while I only wished to erase the day,
especially when, during the cooking of the goat,
Antonio lifted its head from the fire and deftly

sliced off both ears, portions of great honor.
One he gave to the red-haired postman, the epileptic
singer of canto hondo, whose difficult singing
often brought on the seizures that terrified

and humiliated him, yet who continued to sing,
so much did he see himself to be the servant
of his music. And the other he presented to me,
to the tall American, the uncomfortable one,

*   *   *

the teacher of his cousin's woman, who had come
this great distance just to eat with them.
The postman saluted and ate the ear as one might
eat a communion wafer. I tasted it, charred

with a bristle of scorched hair, like a pork rind
or potato chip with a bitter taste, so that I soon
slipped the rest into the trash for which action
eight years later I offer this apology, the angular

American, so uncomfortable with joy. Antonio,
I thought so little of you pointing to your ugly
mouth and laughing, as if you had in some way
demeaned yourself, as if you should feel ashamed

for this abundance of pleasure, this party
for the American couple and their baby. What
apology could I now make, the embarrassment
still rankling like a canker? Wherever you are

that hole in your teeth repeats the story
of the party. You have the bright memory;
I the dark one. You have the gift of good times
recalled; I the clarity of having acted badly.

Nothing to be done, no one left to make better.
On the one hand the memory of the skittish goat,
as if it could see the knife days before its throat
was cut, destined to become somebody's dinner.

*   *   *

On the other the memory of the postman after
we had eaten, shyly rising to his feet, his arms
flat to his sides, and singing in his clear voice,
his head lifted, staring out the window above us,

following the path of his song, terror on one side,
humiliation on the other, but never flinching,
his voice quivering as he held the long notes
that could break him, surrendering himself

to a music like sunlight on the distant valley
and terraced hillside where one could see burros
laden with baskets of cherimoyas and Japanese figs,
zigzagging up the paths toward the village.

His task was as hard as scaling those slopes
on his hands and knees, yet he never faltered as he
gave himself up and became the song's creature
so that people clapped and even I, briefly,

put down my bag of nails, and the older Antonio
beat on the table top and the gap between his teeth
became a second grin, became a small black pit,
and, looking, it seemed that I could see myself

peering out of it, the tentative animal trapped
by his own anxiety about the confusion of events,
while the postman plunged ever deeper into his song,
becoming like a lost thing wandering the hillside

*   *   *

of his own music, not even caring where he
found himself at the end, whether still standing
among us or rolling on the floor, frothing
and biting his tongue, staring up at our confused

and anxious faces, emotions which he could
hardly comprehend, for hadn't he come through
a long and perilous journey, and why should we
worry and feel sorry when he felt only pride?

THE DOUBLE

Arriving home late one night, a man
sees himself through his kitchen window,
sees himself standing near his children
arguing with his wife, sees the same

tweed jacket and red tie, the same expression
of perplexity and anger. The man circles
the outside of his house. He is struck
by how his children at best seem only

to tolerate this shadow man, how his wife's
apparent good humor exists only to keep
her husband from falling into irritation,
how her cheerfulness is simply a burden.

The man stares through his windows. Inside,
the children look up from their dinner.
It is the wind, they say. And the wife
glances toward the dark and remarks how

the night is growing colder. And putting
down his fork, her husband is irritated
by their words' distraction and wishes
they would keep silent. The meal ends

and the family disperses—television,
phone calls, and the evening is wound
to its conclusion. Past midnight, the man
stands in the bathroom listening to the wind

*　　　*　　　*

and the leaves hurtling themselves against
the outside of his house. He can almost make
a language from it. But he is bored and his face
in the mirror seems unfamiliar, somebody older

and loveless, for whom sleep is no escape.
He climbs into bed, turns his back to his wife—
he dreams of fighting, he dreams of trucks
roaring their motors throughout the long night.

HOSPITAL WAITING ROOM

Bald, yellow skinned, with only four
long hairs which she cherishes and combs
like guarding four hairs on a grapefruit,

or that young one with maybe half a dozen,
or the skinny one with ten black hairs
hanging past her shoulders, halfhearted

survivors, souvenirs of past life which she
curls and strokes and protects until
still another falls out and she weeps—

three bald women waiting for therapy,
all their attention fixed on these
last bits, these snippets and scraps,

as if these few threads were all that kept
each one a woman, their last remnants
of femininity, combing and washing them,

winding five hairs around a roller—
what is this stuff, this moss on the dome,
this doormat of the brain, which we can

hardly see except reflected in a mirror
but which we feel so defines us? Why
do they keep them? Surely eight hairs

arranged across the skull like a few
strands of spaghetti on a plate, surely
this is worse than no hair at all. But

*   *   *

it is not their decision, it is the world's
which plucks them like plucking petals
from a flower—it loves them, loves them not—

while they, terrified, wait for the answer,
whether to be lifted up with great rejoicing
or cast down as litter on a barber's floor.

FEET

The brave, the beaten, the shameful ones—
so the body also demands its cowards
and the feet step up, plucked chickens

condemned to the dirt, ten stubby noses
sniffing out danger. Quick, something big
is coming, something fierce is coming.

And so the body trots away. Brave feet
would mean nobody left to talk about it.
Romantic feet, ambitious feet, greedy feet—

all plain dangerous. Best to put a coward
at the wheel. My mother sometimes complains
about what she calls nervous feet, a tingling

in the skin when she sits or tries to read.
Then my brother got it and now I have it too:
a nervous electricity, the feet needing

to exercise themselves as if they sensed death
poised like a hand over the house.
The feet know he's there. They train for it.

That's why they love dancing—heavy drums,
fast music and feet ranging across the floor.
As in that movie where the great general

draws battle plans in the dirt with a stick
so the feet when dancing seem to plot out
elaborate forms of escape. Oh, what a ballet

*　　　*　　　*

it will be—they'll leap up as death ducks down,
they'll dodge left as death jumps right.
Death the male dancer and those shy feet

in their swan costume, spinning, spinning,
until death presses his hand against the most
fragile part of their spine and they tilt

back and farther back and the drums roll—
this is the instant they always prepare for,
twirling and leaping, but escape, there is no

escape, and they chuckle at the romantic conceit
of such a thought before they get back to work,
their fear seduced and abandoned by the aesthetic

appeal of the last moment, intending to get each
contortion just right, imagining the audience's
final roar, the curtain descending on its chains.

THE BODY'S REPOSE AND DISCONTENT

Sometimes the body needs to collect
and recollect itself. Although not quite
a bathtub, it reclines like a bathtub:
head raised, feet up and the belly

balanced like a bucket in between. Those
who know how to sing do, those who can't
hum the best they can, while across the mind's
big screen float images of earthly possessions:

first the dear ones, the red car with new tires,
a raccoon skin coat, a microwave oven
with a tiny TV over the controls
for easy viewing as well as easy cooking.

Then come the shots of what one would like
to buy next—what one thinks of as needs—
a bigger red car, a cottage at the beach,
which lead one to brood on what one lacks.

Here the body grows less happy, the water
in the metaphoric tub turns chilly,
because along with what one lacks comes also
what needs fixing, what's lost or merely missing,

and the list lengthens and the deeds required
to improve the situation seem so desperate
that one begins to recall instead all the people
one thinks one loves and who love in return,

*   *   *

or who owe one a favor. And across the mind's
big screen appears a procession of faces—
the spouse or lover, the kids and old folks—
those sparkling eyes and wide grins which exist

to make one glad. But then come the friends who
haven't called, the acquaintances who have grown
indifferent, the strangers who have been rude,
the enemies for whom one's death wouldn't be sad,

and once again all grows dark and in escape
one turns one's thoughts to food as visions
of comestibles amble across the brain—lobster
Thermidor, steak Diane and apricot cake.

But then, inevitably, come all those delights
one hasn't had, the hippo steaks and hummingbird
tongues one craves to taste, followed once again
by all one lacks until it seems that hunger

has always been one's enemy and that seafood salad
makes one sick and how one has never liked bananas.
So it rolls round and round and each thought
slides toward discontent, the flip side of hope,

the knife point in the back that prods one's feet,
urges one to get busy, until again the organism
heaves itself upright and resumes its journey—
buying, trading, loving, making. Discontent

*   *   *

forms the harness which each person straps on,
and like an army of ancient Egyptians dragging
a giant rock so we are linked to the earth:
each of us grips an invisible rope and we pull.

This is what causes the earth to twinkle
while the sun bounces off its indentations.
Through discontent we make it go, just so
some god someplace can watch it sparkle.

CEZANNE'S AMBITION

He hungered for the fame of Bouguereau,
his country's best loved painter, but distrusted
how such ambition touched his art, and so
to toughen himself with irony and feel disgusted
with his wish for public acclamation he bought
a parrot and taught it to repeat as he worked: Cézanne
is a great painter, which joke gave him the doubt
to paint for the painting itself. But critical scorn
and public mockery hurt him and around that time
he painted *The House of the Hanged Man* with its tangle
of sharp angles, winter trees, thick walls of stone,
the labyrinthine flecks of green, the triangles
like knives around a wedge of country, and a scrap
of blue sky stretching above it—oh, blesséd escape.

CEZANNE'S A MODERN OLYMPIA–*1872*

Most women frightened him, their breasts, their beauty,
their fierce smiles, so he withdrew behind his beard
and black hat, behind his art, and felt his duty
was to his uncompromised gift, and the few nudes
he painted were thick and faceless, more color
and mass than objects of desire, for he felt
too shy to hire female models, had a horror
of laughter, painted his wife and expected to fail.
But an early painting, nearly a cartoon, details
a woman of wonderful pinkness and plumpness
reclining on a white divan, as a great Negress
rises above her removing the last of her veils,
while before her on a pink sofa obviously at ease
rests Cézanne himself unblushing and released.

CEZANNE'S MONTAGNE SAINTE-VICTOIRE

Observing Cézanne's paintings of this mountain
Rilke said, "Nobody has seen a mountain like that
since Moses." But Rilke was mistaken. It wasn't
simply a mountain Cézanne was staring at.
Imagine him spending year after year in a town
where people thought him crazy and mocked him,
and his neighbors gossiped and he had no friends,
while his family complained and he mistrusted them.
Yet each day he went out and gathered up the ugly,
the unpromising or plain, which he stubbornly joined
within his eye and began to paint. But constantly
as if to toughen himself he painted this mountain,
a slope-shouldered pile of stone, bald as a skull,
as if painting himself, painting his stony will.

LAUGHTER

As a pair of hands can stretch a rubber band
so a joke can expand the duration
of a given second, and into that gap,

between the fixed and flexible, we hurry
to insert a barking, choking noise,
which signifies the gift of extra life;

and we feel better knowing we have stolen
another moment, that the predetermined
minutes of our lives have been increased,

and that death, while not beaten, has been dealt
an injury, a minuscule bruise. So eager
are we to find occasions for our laughter

that we rush to stick it in ill-suited places,
for instance when we are nervous or scared,
or when the absurd strikes us with the world's

harsh peculiarity, or even as a weapon,
laughing just to hurt somebody else,
somebody we even care about or love.

Each day begins with a little practice—
the man coughing and clearing his throat
immediately on rising is preparing himself,

the woman gargling and blowing her nose
is getting ready. Our lives are too brief
by half. Can't laughter mean another year,

*   *   *

an extra decade? Think of Methuselah, funniest man
in the ancient world. Think of the centenarians
in rest homes, hacking and chortling, slapping

their plastic knees as the funeral wagons
remove the dour and sour-hearted. And once
when I was strolling in the woods, I decided

that when we die we all return as crows.
It was late fall and snowing slightly.
Off in the distance a mob of crows began

cawing wildly and it sounded like laughter—
those hoarse rasping shouts like sausage slices
cut from the infinite, that frantic chewing of the air,

that rapid propulsion and inhalation of the soul—
black shapes grouped in winter trees,
trying to snatch something of their lives back.

MARCH MORNING

It could never fly—the heart in its cage—
more like a chicken in an oven, plucked
and shivering behind the ribs, stuttering

its two beat song over and over. But still
the heart yearns to fly, yearns to be up there
with the others doing elaborate cartwheels

through the sunlight, tweedling those abstruse
melodies about sex and the mystery of eggs.
What sort of bird would it be if once again

it were covered with feathers? Something green
with the benign machine gun attack and ricochet
of the cardinal; something that hated shadow,

that loved the space above the tree tops. As today
much in the way that dull-witted Cro-Magnon man
must have danced when he hit upon the obligatory

roundness of the wheel, so the birds all cavort
as if they had invented spring, and my heart too
feels up there in desire, as it beats against

the bars of its cage, motivating the legs,
activating the feet. Is this how we walk,
stumbling foot by foot with our shoe leather

nuzzling the dirt, each step a basic failure
of muscle, while the heart heaves us upward,
with lips pursed to kiss the glistening air?

NOSES

Little emissary to tomorrow,
the nose precedes us into the future,
reaching the next moment a moment before us,
a delicate Columbus of uncharted seas.
How brave is its unguarded fragility:
quick to sniffle, easily broken,
ever ready with its shout of warning,
the sneeze. True, the foot may get there
first, but it is cushioned by the shoe
and so for it the world remains abstract.
But the nose—tiny rosebud of the mole,
gallumphing snout of the moose, bump
of the skunk, smidgin of the frog—
easier to imagine a heaven full of noses,
than one full of people, clouds packed
with those soft triangles of flesh.

So this morning I watch my wife's nose
as she sleeps, my fingers hovering
inches above it only to stroke it.
If it were just a matter of noses,
her nose and mine,
how could we ever quarrel or fight?
No harsh words or angry looks.
How could there be anything but love
between those sweet upside-down heart shapes?

ECHOES

With her tight black leotard a second skin
across her chest and her skirt a thin ribbon
around her thighs, she lingers in the doorway

of the men's weight room, arching her back,
raising her arms to knit her fingers
behind her head, until her ribs climb

like ladders toward her breasts, and the men
respond with grunts and sweat, their muscles
pressing against the skin, pushing toward her

as if they could burst from their bodies
to lie at her feet, which is a fantasy she likes,
the muscles becoming unfleshed and yearning

instead of hidden, their labors unrecognized,
the body's proletariat, its blue collar section.
But here in the weight room they bulge and glisten

and she could do without the rest, the man's brain
and male desires, the smells and hair, like a brute's,
and muscular herself and sure of her good looks

she has come to speak to them, enliven them,
to winnow them from their anatomy for they form
her own sweet study, and pressed to the door frame,

lifting her breasts, she resembles a climber
on a cliff face calling across a deep valley
and the muscles grunt, their maleness discarded

*   *   *

like chaff, and their stretching and sweating
becomes the echo she is seeking, her own voice
returned to her, but no longer small, a voice

like a hundred reflections, so that wherever
she turns and casts her eye, she finds herself
answering back, lovingly and full of desire.

THE MUSIC ONE LOOKS BACK ON

In early autumn, there's a concerto
possible when there's a guest in the house
and the guest is taking a shower and the host
is washing up from the night before.
With each turn of the tap in the kitchen,
the water temperature increases or drops
upstairs and the guest responds with little groans—
cold water for low notes, hot water for high.
His hair is soapy, the tub slippery
and with his groaning he becomes the concerto's
primary instrument. Then let's say the night
was particularly frosty and now the radiators
are knocking, filling the house with warmth,
and the children are rushing around outside
in the leaves before breakfast, calling after
their Irish setter whose name is Cleveland.
And still asleep, the host's wife is making
those little sighs one makes before waking,
as she turns and resettles and the bed creaks.
Standing at the sink, the host hums to himself
as he thinks of the eggs he'll soon fry up,
while already there's the crackle of bacon
from the stove and a smell of coffee. The mild groans
of the guest, the radiator's percussion,
children's high voices, the barking of a dog,
even the wife's small sighs and resettlings
combine into this autumn concerto of which
not one of the musicians is aware as they drift
toward breakfast and then a leisurely walk
through the fields near the house—two friends

who haven't seen each other for over a year.
Much later they will remember only a color,
a golden yellow, and the sound of their feet
scuffling the leaves. A day without rancor
or angry words, the sort of day that builds a life,
becoming a soft place to look back on,
and geese, geese flying south out of winter.

SHAVING

It is really the most minuscule thing,
but you see sometimes when I shave,
my daughter follows me into the bathroom
to watch—she's sixteen months—and each
time she insists that I take the brush,
smear it around the lather in the cup,
then dab a small lump onto her hand,
which she studies, intently. Some mornings
I must do this five or six times before
I'm done scraping the remnants of yesterday
from my face. The brush is from a past life,
the present of an ex-girlfriend, and it's
at least ten times my daughter's age.
As for the badger, whose bristles
we are sharing, it must have been Swiss,
like the brush, and long turned to dust.
But I watch my daughter in the glass
and her pleasure seems so simple that I
don't mind the bother as she pokes
the lather, sniffs it, tastes it and
smears it over her hands and face up there
on the third floor of the house where I
shave in a small bathroom without windows.
I am forty-five. I had never thought,
actually, that to have a child at my age
would be different than any other age.
Probably, I'm even more patient. But
I think how in twenty years when she
is getting started, I'll be checking out,
that is, if all goes right between times.

Let them keep it, I've always thought.
Let them fend off the impending collapse.
But you know those parties where late at night
the whole place starts busting apart—
too many arguments, too many fights,
and you're just as glad to get moving,
that's how I always thought I would feel,
stepping into the big zero, but now
I see I'll be abandoning my daughter
there in the midst of the recklessness:
the bully with grabby hands, the lout
eager to punch somebody out, and my daughter,
who, in these musings while I shave,
is still under three feet tall and poking
at the lather smeared across her hand.
I joke, you know, I say we're raising her
to be the girlfriend of a Russian soldier,
or next week she'll begin karate lessons
and learn to smash carrots with a single blow.
But it all comes back as I watch her
in the mirror. Who is going to protect her?
Even now anything could happen. Last summer,
for instance, I rented a cottage from a fellow
who had a place up the hill, and one day I heard
these bees whipping past me, and you know what?
It was him, my landlord, fooling with his .22,
shooting beer cans off a wall with me strolling around
down below. But that's how it is all the time,
the load of bricks crashing behind us
as the flower pot smashes at our feet.
And cancer and car accidents, everyone's

got stories. How can I not think of this
when I watch my daughter messing
with the shaving lather? The whole
world gets vague and insubstantial, like
putting your finger through a wet tissue,
the muggers, rapists, terrorists, the Bomb.
It's just luck whether you escape or get hit,
making you feel about as safe as a light bulb
in a hailstorm which, of course, is exactly
how it is, except worse. But to have a child
means to expand the dimensions of the dark place,
until I wind up imagining this small
blindfolded creature toddling out on a rope
over the abyss and it's my daughter, my daughter,
this sweet morsel left over at the violent party,
this Russian girlfriend of the future. Well,
some mornings such thoughts crowd in on me
when I go upstairs to shave, and she
comes toddling after. That lather is so soft,
such a fragile conglomeration of white bubbles,
such a minuscule smidgin of possibility,
maybe that's why she likes it, dabbing it
with one finger, lifting it up, right there
by the pink ceramic toilet and torn green
shower curtain with silhouettes of fish,
sniffing this small heap of white bubbles,
touching it to her nose, then puff, just
blowing gently, so the bubbles hang, floating,
floating, and then they're gone of course.

DELICIOUS MONSTROSITY

With the flat side of white plastic spatulas
three old ladies perch on a park bench, slapping
gobs of blackberry jam onto slabs of dark bread.

Nearby a hobo snoozing on the grass spots the women
and thinks just how sweet that jam would taste.
He gets to his feet, but the women do not see him.

It is about to rain, but the women do not notice.
The park will soon be torn up to make room
for a parking lot, as was reported in the papers,

but the women have no interest in the papers.
And the world, that delicious monstrosity,
what is happening within its sweet confusion?

Unfortunately, the women haven't the foggiest.
Oh, the tart smoky taste of blackberry jam,
that syrupy glop of pleasure on the tongue,

and the one perfect moment stretched out like
the stretched elastic bands of a sling shot,
until there comes the hard crack of the day

being disrupted, like the sound of a rock
smacking a window. The women scream, people turn.
Has something gone wrong? What can be seen?

Only a shabby man, in stolen clothes, doing
a little dance as he swiftly departs, licking
drops of blackberry jam from his unshaven lips.

THE FUTURE

Next day, next week, next year,
why not think of the future
as a fat man with a thick stick?
He swings his stick—bam goes a tree.
He swings it again—bam goes somebody's cow.
This is the fellow we are trying to sneak by.
Sometimes he sleeps, sometimes he counts his money.
And we, we spend our lives on tiptoe,
scurrying around hushing our neighbors—
a sound often taken for the sound of the sea.
Nevertheless, without a scrap of reason, we remain
optimistic. Everything will be okay, we say.
Is this what makes us so endearing,
that our hope persists against all odds?
And if, in our infinite cleverness,
we manage to sneak past his dogs, tripwires,
his constant anger, a complete encyclopedia
of horrors, even if we slide by unnoticed,
we plunge at once into a thick fog. No noise,
nothing around us, no eyes to see with,
nose to sniff with, no ears to hear with,
lips to kiss with, no feet to dance with,
knees to knock with, no legs to run with.
And just before it all becomes clear—
Safe at last, we shout, but is nobody there?

FINGERNAILS

Little excavators, postage stamps
of living stone, you seek to save me
from the encroaching dust—scratch it away,

scratch it away. Do you think if I stood
long enough in one spot, the earth itself
would bury me: wave after wave

of tiny particles, bits of dirt,
until with nobody's help I'd be
six feet under? But you would free me,

or try to, for what can you really do,
diminished claws, dwarfish shovels
against the future? It is not your ability

one cherishes, but your rudimentary
fidelity, sacrificing all to this body
of which you are the true frontier.

No wonder one hears how you scream
when the torturers try to take you from us.
You should be perilous, the body's own

outlaw band, each finger a pistol,
each nail a flashing scimitar,
but you're small: trifling talons

with which to attack a pimple,
petite mirrors incapable of reflecting.
Yet when death's broom sweeps me

*　　　*　　　*

into the ground, you'll keep growing
believing you can scratch your way back
to the surface. Wake up, you might say,

we're still here, we're ready to dig—
while the silence answers with more silence
and a beetle shoves a pebble up a hill.

THE BODY'S JOY

The slick kiss of an oyster slipping
across the tongue, a woman's bare thighs
with her belly a velvet lake beneath
one's hands, warm wind in spring, a change
in the weather, the touch of silk, sleep—

these become the body's joy: a fire
on a cold night, good brandy, the separation
of a zipper, the senses all opening
like ornate doors through which the world
passes in its pumpkin carriage. The body

has a hunger to wallow in such moments
and hunts them out through a dark forest
of coffin lids and grandfather clocks.
But not the mind: for it the perfect moment
is the moment before, the drop of honey

elongating above the tongue, and so the mind
sorts through a series of alternative futures
before selecting some distant object—sex,
money, power—to activate work's narcotic,
desire's fur mitten, ambition's limousine.

Both mind and body seek to discover whatever
defeats the steady gallop of time, whatever
distracts from the world's devastation of moments,
so time itself can be made to dance like a ball
balancing on a spume of water in the sunlight.

*　　　*　　　*

Both seek to fracture the minuscule chamber
of each second, not to be bound by the one
door to the past or the other to the future,
but to create a third door, the best door,
opening onto an eternal present—a place

without guilt, regret or the prospect of pain.
Summer lawns slope down to a river where late
afternoon light sparkles on the water. We hear
the muted voices of our friends playing croquet,
women's laughter and meat sizzling on a grill.

Off to the south all is dark, and to the north
the clouds are heaping up. There will be a storm,
but not yet, not yet. The slackening day beckons,
our feet sink into the soft grass, our friends
turn to greet us. For this impossible second,

that is ending even as we begin it, the world
becomes complete: our joy like a dragonfly poised
on a leaf, the moist touch of a glass against our lips,
a barn swallow that twists and flits, a bright
flung thing caught in the vanishing light.

CEZANNE'S DOUBTS

He was a hard painter to pose for. Hours stuck
in the same spot, while he grumbled and fussed,
up to a hundred sittings till his nerves broke
and he junked the canvas and heaped abuse
on the unlucky model, friend or wife,
who had sat for weeks for absolutely no point.
His still lives took so long the flowers died,
forcing him to use paper flowers, wax fruit.
And so he would often paint himself. Only he
had the persistence to outlast his gaze,
but in each case something lies behind the calm,
perhaps a question or trace of uncertainty,
not of some weakness of his eye, but surprise
at the grim and outcast creature he had become.

CEZANNE'S FORTRESS

His clothing smelled, he rarely washed, often grumbling
or cursing, eager to argue, ready to fight,
"a bear," he called himself, "an obstinate macrobite,"
and so he withdrew behind the walls of his painting.
Unable to talk without tumbling into a fury,
tongue-tied before women, uncertain with men,
quick to weep at a kind word, frequently sullen,
he protected himself behind a fortress of beauty.
There his life was well-spoken, properly dressed;
his art became his own version of articulateness,
meant to show his true nature. "The most tantalizing
feature of painting," he wrote, "is the character
of the artist himself." And the critics kept taunting:
"The triflings of a savage, the daubs of a trash collector."

CEZANNE'S FAILURE

His doubt made him impossible to live with.
How hard to possess the only voice that knows
how and what to paint but can't. His faith
needed constant help and he was a terror to please.
"There's only one living painter—myself," he declared.
And so he lived alone, nursed his ferocity,
grew cheap and found exploitation everywhere.
"All my compatriots are pigs compared to me,"
he wrote in his last letter to his son.
But still he swore to die painting, while hating
what he perceived as failure, that he could never attain
the intensity of the world he saw unfolding
before his senses, saying, "I paint with pleasure
but lack the wealth of color that animates nature."

TRAFFIC

Crains, dans le mur aveugle, un
regard qui t'pie
      —GERARD DE NERVAL

I was driving to pick up my daughter from day care.
It was a summer afternoon and hot, just rush hour
and traffic was terrible, all jam-packed and scarcely

moving ten feet before the light changed again,
crammed in with the hesitant, the nervous,
the cretins of forward locomotion. Of course

I was in a hurry as were the people around me.
But as we stopped again I heard a radio blaring,
and glancing into the car on my left I saw

two men slouched in front and the one closest
was singing to the music, just mouthing the words.
They looked like construction workers or maybe

they cut lawns or dug ditches, something outside—
two men in their mid-twenties. The song blasting
across the intersection was "Stairway to Heaven,"

a big song of the early seventies by Led Zeppelin,
a song that starts with a lot of restraint,
then goes crazy. More importantly it's a song

about transcendence, the spiritual world
that exists beneath the mundane. The young man
was unshaven and fat. Seeing him, the word

*   *   *

that leapt to mind was lummox. Yet what caught
my attention was the man's expression
as he sang—it showed such a wistful yearning,

such tenderness, the child rising to the surface
in the face of the adult. And with the yearning
was the suspicion he knew full well he was a lummox,

that his spirit was trapped in a fat body, stuck
in a rusty Ford in a heat wave in midsummer.
All this was the perception of a second.

I heard the music, saw the young man mouthing
the words, saw his expression of yearning, then
traffic moved forward and the man was replaced

by a woman chewing gum. But this also happened:
here I was jammed together with my enemies,
people no better than chunks of wood, impediments

to my dinner, as I was an impediment to theirs.
And actually the man in the next car looked like
the sort you stay away from in a bar, the fat boy

with a grudge, only too happy to punch your head.
Yet in that wistful reaching out his whole being
took shape. How can I describe the impression

of an instant—to despise my fellow creatures,
then to notice the lummox singing like a stone
become a flower, to feel my heart begin to ache

*　　　*　　　*

as if the breath were about to burst from my body,
as if we were all reaching toward shadow selves
that hurry ahead above the road, blowing like the stuff

of a dandelion clock, or wisps of cloud or smoke,
this bit of light the lummox was reaching out for,
which he saw disappearing while he stayed trapped

in traffic in his mortal lummoxy body, as if always
there is the lummox self and the shadow self,
sometimes close, sometimes impossibly distant,

but more, still more, as if this shadow self
contained all he was and all he wanted to be,
graceful and light and unrestricted, while he

in his lummox body was simply a mud shape
slapped together by a careless child. All this
was written in his face—that his burden

was the knowledge of this separation. But who
did I see, seeing this man, and what did I catch
but a glimpse, a snippet picked up through a crack

in the wall? Because then the cars moved forward
and I went straight and he turned left and I never
saw him again—cars dividing and rejoining

like clouds dispersing across the sky. Remember
as a child lying in the grass, watching the sky
and the clouds flung about there? What shapes

*   *   *

they promised as the clouds ordered themselves
and came together with suggestions of meaning,
until one could almost see the unifying pattern,

some animal or face one thought one knew, but then
they scattered again, rushed off to all corners.
Yet that hint of connection was so telling

that in looking I felt on the brink of falling
and I would thrust my fingers into the grass
and hang there, arching my back and quick of breath.

UTOPIAN MELODIES

As a stone has a sense of its hardness,
or steel of its hardness, so this man,
the department's most severe post-structuralist,
feels all the world's books buffet against him
and fall away. Walking, he tilts forward
tightly clenched as if fighting a stiff wind.
It forms his duty to the future to overturn
the lies of the past. And what lies:
the anger of Achilles, the madness of Lear;
rather fabrications patched together by minds
which had removed their attention from the plain
truths of the world, aspiring instead
to impotent godhood. But like a stone this man
is made of the world and the world is made
from his body and the world will tolerate
no lie. Even language has betrayed him, being
like smoke, not stone, and so he will reinvent it
just as he intends to remake all things.
His Eden will have a chainlink fence. Little
will grow there, nothing flower, for what is beauty
but the arch deceiver, something to snatch
one's heart for a few seconds, filling it
with light, before returning it to a world
which has grown darker. His ambition is for
a single emotion, a wintry one, and no lies,
a life focused like a microscope upon a virus,
and from his studies he will fashion a music
from metal being twisted and breaking glass.

MORNING NEWS

Searching for bugs, rolling in the grass,
the children explore the field this first
warm morning in spring—ages five, six
and sixteen months. Clio eats a leaf
while Emery imparts misinformation to Amiel
as if that's what growing up were all about,
not knowledge but the sophistication of ignorance.
Behind me the radio describes the wounded day
while from the front porch I watch the children
sit in their circle as in a round boat
made of sticks. How happily they discuss
the improbable world as their boat drifts
farther toward deep water till there is only
their bright chatter as wisps of fog shift
like tattered cloth and soon the foghorns blow.

WALLS TO PUT UP,
WALLS TO TAKE DOWN

The old madhouse in Santiago stood tucked back
behind the hospital on a side street to the cemetery,
walls of cheap brick, cheap concrete through which
the inmates had bored little holes, and walking past

one could see dozens of cleft sticks with notes
offered to the passersby, some begging for money,
others for help or food, some asking that word be sent
to some friend or relative or lover who surely

must be waiting just as they themselves had waited,
all day holding their sticks as if fishing over
a dry pond, the water seeped away, leaving several
tires, a cat skeleton tied to a brick, a rusted

car door. I remembered all this in a hotel bar
in Belgrade when a whore was telling me, "My name
is Dragonova but I prefer to be called Lolita."
Lolita the promise, Dragonova the reality,

a beautiful girl hoping to become a hairdresser,
but no matter how much I wanted her flesh, to cup
her breasts, nuzzle my nose in her belly, it was
her flesh that stood between us and what I wanted,

stood between us like the wall of the madhouse.
"A little pop," a friend said, "you should have
taken her upstairs for a little pop." But what
could we really do? She might charitably moan.

*   *   *

I might have my little flash of light, a meal
after which one still feels hungry. The thing is
that nobody ever went down that street in Santiago.
It was a side street. But it didn't matter, it was

the only street they had. Sometimes with my wife,
if we haven't been quarreling, it feels like
we are sitting together without skin, a large basket
of confused body parts. "In this mood," as Wordsworth

remarked, "successful composition generally begins."
It's as if I could reach her skin from the inside,
burrowing outward instead of poking at the surface
like a dowser looking for water. Flaubert in Egypt

had a wonderful whore, Kuchuk Hanem, who he swore
would remember him more than all the others.
"Toward the end," he wrote, "there was something
sad and loving about the way we touched."

Later he realized his self-deception. "This
particular tourist who was vouchsafed the honors
of her couch has vanished from her memory like
all the others." Also, "As for physical pleasure,

it must be slight, since the famous button, the seat
of such pleasure, is snipped off at an early age."
And he concludes, "Traveling makes one modest—
you see what a tiny spot you inhabit in the world."

*　　*　　*

And as a postscript: "I must tell you, my dear sir,
that I picked up in Beirut (I discovered them in Rhodes,
land of the dragon) seven chancres . . . Each night
and morning I bandage my poor prick." Recently,

in Santiago I went searching for this madhouse
and it was gone, torn down, and only a section
of wall remained through which the inmates
had pushed their sticks. A hot and smoggy day,

the streets crowded with buses, cabs. Think of
all those people in transit—all those destinations
with one single destination waiting a little further
beyond. The mental patients, more like prisoners,

had been transferred. Or perhaps with modern medicine
they had been released and had no need to ask
for anything, plead or beg for anything, as they
proceeded in speedy transition from one less

than perfect place to the next. Do you remember
how Ford Madox Ford wrote that you marry a person
to finish a conversation with her? And I also
like how that summons up that somewhat outdated

legal expression for illicit fucking: criminal
conversation, or crim con as they said in the courts.
Many times my wife and I speak only to complain
and I am the bag of stones she wears around her neck,

*   *   *

but other times, fewer times, we are engaged in that
long conversation, the one we stay together for,
the one we always hope for, where the flesh seems
to disappear and the parts get all jumbled together

as in a cannibal's stew, even if she sits in one chair
and I sit in another. The whore in Belgrade knew
about one hundred words in English and half were
the specialty words of her profession. I bought her

a Coke. She asked why I was in Belgrade. In explanation
I showed her the book of my poems translated into
her language. She read a few, decided she wanted it,
asked for it, asked me to sign it, then carried it

off to her next customer, beautiful skimpily dressed
girl with a face of shadow and a book of poems.
Oh, Dragonova/Lolita sleep with it under your pillow
just once. Those inmates in Santiago could see nothing,

hear nothing. All they had were those holes and their
messages—help me, they put me here by mistake—
and years of waiting until the whole place was
torn down. And I asked my wife who knew the city,

Didn't you ever read the messages? And she said,
No one ever stopped. Some friends had told her what
the bits of paper said. At the end of the street
stood the huge granite gates of the cemetery, like

*   *   *

the gates of a municipal museum but bigger, a city
of corpses with its ghettos and rich neighborhoods,
rows of fancy houses although no one asks to borrow
a cup of sugar. The trouble with Belgrade, the promise

of Lolita and the actuality of Dragonova, her mad-
house walls and my madhouse walls rubbing crazily
together, what if I grew to like it? It makes me
remember an old Texan in Amsterdam in 1959—

for us teenagers the lovely Dutch whores charged
two dollars and seventy cents if any of us managed
to dredge up the nerve, for this Texan they charged
twenty-seven dollars and a lot of laughter. Still

he would stagger out each evening, his guts hurt,
kidneys hurt, his prick was wobbly and battered
as he kept banging himself against the hard Dutch flesh.
Sometimes around midnight I would find him in a bar

too depressed even to speak. He had children
somewhere, a divorced wife. What beauty gives us
is the hope of intimacy. Fashion and advertising,
the whole package, all promise a certain closeness,

an occasion when the walls might disappear,
one inmate rubbing his belly against another
belly of his choosing, or which has chosen him,
the long conversation, the erasure of isolation,

*   *   *

as if we might all be piled together like puppies
in a pet shop window, a tangle of extremities
and no barriers anyplace, hardly any need to speak,
each thought anticipated and responded to,

no concern for the future, no regret for the past,
just this complete touching, this discourse
with all the barriers gone, and that's the joke,
right? Who put the walls up in the first place,

who made them indestructible and now we want them
gone? I told my wife, can you take me to that street?
So we drove through Santiago. Smog so dense
our eyes burned, but all we found were just fragments

of brick walls with little holes bored through them,
thick walls, nearly two feet of boring and digging,
then the waiting, occasionally jiggling the stick
to show someone was there, and we knew without speaking

they hadn't been released, weren't out on the street,
but that somewhere were new walls of red brick
or concrete, and on one side someone was trying to scratch
his way through with a pin to make a hole

big enough for a little note, a little request,
and on the other side the traffic, the honking,
air so thick with fumes it wipes out the mountains,
leaving just the city, its constant jittery motion.

HOW IT WAS AT THE END

The box was set in a hole in the ground,
a white cardboard box big enough
for a corsage, in a hole big enough for a rose bush.
It was raining; a few prayers were said.
And his granddaughter said, How did they make him so little
to put him in such a little box?
And her cousin said, How do you mean, they burned him?
A few people sprinkled dirt over the box,
but an hour later it still stood uncovered,
growing sodden as the hole filled with water.
My wife showed it to me, then went to look for a shovel.
But there was no shovel, no trowel or big spoon.
We scooped up the mud with our hands
and piled it onto the white cardboard, just enough
to cover it. Then we wiped our hands on the grass—
thick, gloppy, turd-colored, mud-smelling mud—
rubbing hard. But still we found it stuck between
our fingers or under the nails, flecks of dirt
which we picked at throughout the long afternoon.
That was three days ago and the rain keeps falling.
It is October. The leaves make their bright passage
from the trees to that nothingness called eternal.

BLACK GIRL VANISHING: DETROIT, 1970

When the truck crawled up from the river,
the driver had no thought that the street
would be full of protest: a peace march gone

unpeaceful, hundreds of the mostly young
blocking rush hour traffic along Jefferson—
a huge tractor trailer with the name Chrysler

painted on the side. He saw them; they saw him,
and the single moment increased itself,
like a balloon pumped full of air. Meanwhile,

five hundred drivers waited impatiently
in five hundred stalled cars and the truck
was the one thing moving, a movement which

burst the expanded moment, because he wasn't
obeying the rules, was meant to stand still
like everyone else, only he didn't know it.

Somebody yelled, Get the pig. Then others shouted
and dozens of the athletic and angry rushed
toward the truck, which created for the driver

another moment, a shorter one. He was slowly
pulling onto Jefferson, a young man in a red cap,
and he stared at these people who had just

made him the focus of all their frustration,
and abruptly over the shouting and random honking
came the harsh roar of the truck's motor

*   *   *

as the driver jammed his foot to the floor
and the truck lurched up Jefferson, both
doors locked and already the cab covered

with the quickest and most nimble, meaning
to catch this guy, drag him into the street
for Cambodia and Kent State, while all the driver

hoped to do was get home, have a beer, watch
some TV, tickle his daughter, whatever, the usual
after work folderol; and as he shifted to second

the righteously indignant began falling away
like bees off a bear, all of which was only
preparation for the next moment, the main moment,

the one that fixed the day in a thousand histories,
where the Me and the Them and the Those came
together for an instant, then fragmented apart,

because most of us knew the driver was innocent,
were glad to see him get away. But that knowledge
formed a wedge breaking the resolve of the crowd,

since by chasing the truck, now disappearing
up Jefferson, they had weakened the human
barrier still blocking traffic, leaving it

to the small, the slow, the half serious, until
with a screech of tires a dark Cadillac leapt
forward out of line, the driver a gray haired man

*   *   *

with a face like a fist, while stuck to his hood
like a piece of gum was a black girl
in a red mini-skirt, thin, wispy, with eyes

so big that in staring at them one was first
aware only of whiteness. That perception became
the day's primary moment, hardly to be called

a moment since the Cadillac must have been hitting
about forty as it headed for the tunnel beneath
Cobo Hall. But it felt like a section of time

split off from the repeating box cars of many
moments, as we all focused on the girl's eyes,
huge and terrified, a black girl stuck to the hood

like a bag of groceries accidentally left outside,
and no sense of how she was hanging on or why
she didn't hurtle off back into the road,

arms and legs sprawling, a screaming rag doll.
Then they were gone, vanished into the tunnel,
and no one saw her fall, which she must have

given the car's speed and the driver's anger;
and soon it was over, traffic surged forward,
the crowd broke into groups, then smaller groups,

then into separate individuals, turning this way
and that, their sense of purpose fled. The young
and angry becoming the feeble and frustrated,

*   *   *

everyone returning to the business of getting home,
a truncated rebellion, as useful as banging our heads
against a wall, an issue deflected rather

than resolved, interrupted rather than ended,
because twenty years later it still seems the girl
is stuck to the hood, impossible of course,

but the way she disappeared down that hole,
with her huge eyes and the huge anger of the driver,
while we, the impotently indignant, felt we had

placed her there with well-intentioned hands,
placed her on the vehicle of her own destruction,
then left her, while unable to turn completely away,

unable to push her memory from our minds,
unable to claim for ourselves a plausible innocence,
unable to end the violence or join its victims,

left only to retreat uncertainly to the curb,
unable to hinder, unable to help: and still
the indifferent traffic keeps roaring past.

INAPPROPRIATE GESTURES

A butcher glances through a bank window and sees
a holdup in progress. Grabbing his backpack,
he thrusts bratwurst at the first ten people he meets.

A baker is witness to a dreadful murder. Two thugs
kill a nun with a folding chair. The baker dials
the zoo and asks how long the zebra has been sick.

A candlestick maker comes home to find her hubby
in bed with a floozy. Horrified, she snatches up
their Irish setter and hurls it into the Jacuzzi.

We are surrounded by inappropriate gestures.
The house is on fire. Quick, grab a tomato!
Bobby fell in the well. Hurry, play the trombone!

Let's say there was a plague or terrible war.
Everywhere people would be pulling on galoshes,
dancing the two-step, buying rabbits like crazy.

These gestures keep the future at a distance,
like a painted backdrop of cows and green fields
to hang between us and the fixed course of events.

But time is like a fat man at a banquet table—
he gobbles up the future and shits it into the past.
If we listen, we can even hear him chewing: days come,

days gone, days come, days gone. Who will save us?
We are lackluster virgins which the mustachioed world
ties to the train tracks of tomorrow's locomotive.

TOTING IT UP

He bought one pair of boots, then another.
They were good boots. He had a four boots life.
He bought twelve cars. He had a twelve car life.

He had fifty-three hundred orgasms but hungered
for a few hundred more. He had two wives:
a two wife life, a four kids life, a twelve

grandchildren life. He drank thirty-four thousand
six hundred and sixty-six cups of coffee.
He ate a quarter of a ton of spaghetti.

He had five heart attacks: a five heart attack life.
He was in the hospital ten times. He had
a two cane life, a one pair of crutches life

a one wheelchair life, a one final illness life,
and all his memories vanished like bubbles
from a glass of champagne. His last suit of clothes

turned to dust and his coffin turned to dust
more slowly. To his grandchildren he was a face,
to their children a name and to their children

a vacancy, and over his grave a road was built,
and the world rolled down that road. See there
in the distance, that brightly disappearing speck.

SWEAT

Lachrymae of the body, for whom do you weep?
What are your griefs, fears? Do you have a favorite
someplace whom violent motion makes you remember?
Does exertion bring her figure to mind and you sob?

Or is it for stasis that you mourn, complete
inaction, no past, no future, all muscles at rest.
Or are these drops not tears but the celebration
of the body's flavor: as a roast in the oven

will exude droplets of juice, so the body
in exertion is always cooking? Or perhaps
you are liquid refreshment, the body's nectar,
so that I should run and jump, then scrape myself

with a wineglass and drink a toast. Here's
to myself—sweet days, sweet nights and the salt
taste of sweat. But no, these drops are tears.
Exertion or heat make the body recollect

what it strives to forget, eventual immobility,
the grave's invitation, as if the body
in motion were bedeviled by contrast—action
reminding it of inaction, time of time's

completion, which leads the body to remember
those days when, pink and smelling of talcum,
its movements were the focus of all attention,
and its parents bent over it with moony smiles

*   *   *

and gentle pats, leading it once again to thoughts
of extinction, as if the body were truly baking,
and death the moment when it is taken from the oven.
For whom does the body in motion weep? It weeps

for itself and the tears roll from its forehead
and the shirt sticks to its back, and dark circles,
like circles under the eyes after a sleepless night,
dark circles stain its clothes beneath the armpits.

THE BODY'S STRENGTH

The mind may not mind death. It means
at last letting go, the inevitable
capitulation. After all, it's tired,
very tired. But the body fights
right to the end. Up, it keeps saying,
you must get up. Think how the body combines
the most improbable collection of parts
from toenail to earlobe, kneecap
to armpit, all with different
functions and desires like a room packed
with the strangest people possible—
rabbit punchers to perfume sippers,
hot dog maniacs to telepathic Chinese,
yet even the smallest pore keeps saying,
Keep moving. One might think the aging body
is like the donkey, while the mind
is like the man with the whip perched
on the overladen cart, but really their wishes
are the opposite with the donkey plodding
dumbly ahead and the man shouting stop.
What keeps it going? What does the body
enjoy? At the end it can hardly hear much,
taste much, see much, smell much and a lot
just hurts, but still the body must delight
in the feel of itself even when it says ouch,
must love the touch of flesh against bones,
like a young girl wearing a silk dress
for the first time. And then it's stubborn,
one foot plopped down after another—
that's how those pyramids got built.

Get a cut, skin closes up; eat some poison,
stomach pukes it out; suffer heartbreak,
the eyes locate a new cutie pretty quick;
get sick and the white cells gang up
to kick the intruder out. Don't stop,
don't stop—the heart a valentine metronome,
a drill sergeant calling out cadence,
the clock hurrying us on to the next second,
but also, luckily, the switch which at last
clicks off, otherwise we would be like turtles
flipped over in the dirt with four feet
pumping the air, pumping the air
and no place left to get to.

CEZANNE'S SECLUSION

"I have begun to think," he wrote in a late letter,
"that one cannot help others at all." This
from a man who once called friendship the highest
virtue. And in another he wrote: "Will I ever
attain the end for which I have striven so long?"
His greatest aspiration was certainty
yet his doubts made him blame himself wrongly,
perceiving each painting a disaster. These swings
between boldness and mistrust, intimacy and isolation
led him to stay at home, keep himself concealed,
becoming a sort of hermit, whose passion for the world
directed every brushstroke, changed each creation
into an expression of tenderness, which he dismissed,
writing: "a vague sense of apprehension persists."

—

CÉZANNE'S LOVE OF POETRY

Nearly friendless, with only a few years to live,
Cézanne committed to memory Baudelaire's poem
"The Carrion" in which the speaker reminds his love
of a corpse they had seen on the road, a woman
with her legs raised in the air like a tart's,
swollen with gas, crawling with maggots and flies,
a dog crouched nearby ready to resume its feast,
and the poet remarks: this will be you when you die.
Cézanne recited this poem as he painted,
finishing his still lives of skulls on a table.
He liked how Baudelaire claimed to have rescued
his lover's essence while the rats squabbled
over her corpse. The poem kept things clear:
like what slips by and what one keeps painting for.

CEZANNE AND THE LOVE OF COLOR

Because his wife refused to miss a dress fitting,
she missed his death instead. He painted to the last,
a portrait in profile of his gardener sitting
in a green light, with a sprawling shadow cast
on the wall behind him. His son too arrived too late,
preferring with his mother the rich life of Paris.
Then, thinking his fame wouldn't last and heavy in debt,
they quickly sold his paintings, foolishly reckless
in their acceptance of small sums. "You see," his wife
told Matisse, "Cézanne couldn't paint. He didn't have
the talent to complete his pictures." Her fear
cost her a fortune. At the very end of his life
Cézanne wrote, "Long live those who have the love
of color—true representatives of light and air."

SURPRISE

As a man with a trowel can smear wet concrete
across a wall, so the years slap age
across our faces, spreading it thick, a puffy
impasto so it seems like something added

to what's already there, the face becoming
inflated, soft, as if it could drip down,
and the cheeks get bigger, the nose bigger
as if the pores had pumped themselves up,

were stretched, made deeper, the craters
of volcanos seen from a plane, everything
additional, a mud pack or rubber mask
laid across the face we had when young

and which can be pulled, stretched, so much
sticky paste, the sloppy glop of papier mache
which hardens and clings and becomes what
the world knows us by and across which time

writes its little notes apropos the lateness
of the day. But the eyes looking out remain
the same eyes, perhaps weaker, perhaps needing
glasses, but it seems they see what they have

always seen, they are the same precise tool,
which allows us to imagine, if we're sitting
absolutely still, that we're plugging along as ever,
and we feel at sixty as we did at twenty, until

*   *   *

something hurls our face back at us, a mirror,
reflections from store windows, water, the glass
over a picture, some shiny surface, the eyes
seek the past, mirrors inflict the present,

as last night in a restaurant glancing across
the room and seeing an older man staring back—who
is this guy, this audacious joker?—and turning
away to avoid his eye, then abruptly gyrating back

and spotting the glass wall, raising my fingers
to my cheeks, nose. Are these my features, my skin?
And with what further disguises and gray
substitutions will the years malign my bones?

INVASIONS

The abrupt presentiment of illness,
the sudden invasion of the foreign:
your wife has been sick, your daughters
sick, and all at once while listening

to a lecture you grow aware of some new
thing within you, something not there
a moment ago. The room fades, the speaker's
voice grows silent, and your whole body

turns inward to discover the intruder,
as you sort through yourself like
searching for a tick on a shaggy dog.
The awareness of a burglar, the intrusion

of a trespasser, a sneeze, a scratchy
feeling in the chest: like being alone
in a house at night, sitting upstairs
reading before the fire and downstairs

there is a sudden noise, a fork falling
to the floor in the kitchen, and every
pore turns to listen, every hair bends
to determine the extent of the invasion.

But this awareness of trespass is also
the reaction to the process of aging—
the pulled muscle, the pain where all was well,
stiffness in the joints, then the diseases,

*   *   *

the inevitable failings, while each daily
humiliation brings with it the sense of how
life used to be: what your feet felt like
before they hurt, what your eyes saw like

before they needed glasses. By itself each
intruder seems small. There's room enough,
you say, as you move your books upstairs.
Then the doorbell rings again and strange cars

fill the driveway, and someone is pounding
at the back, and soon your visitors crowd
the kitchen, invade the downstairs rooms.
Each is starving and still they keep coming.

Soon the rooms are packed, the couches creaking,
then a glass breaks, a chair breaks,
the food is all eaten, the dancing begins,
strange laughter erupts from the bedroom.

Steadily, you are pushed toward the door—
as nobody said hello, neither do they say
au revoir—and soon you are outside, holding
a snapshot of your house as it once was,

before your guests created its present
dilapidation. Someone shouts from a window:
Get lost, get moving! So you set off, hardly
seeing your path as you focus on the picture:

*   *   *

the slate roof, the red brick. And there you are
waving from a window. How handsome you look.
Remember that time? A parade of bright mornings,
waking in a house you thought was yours forever.

TONGUE

Is it you who have destroyed me, sweetness,
small phallus of the mouth, caressing the world
with your knobby surface—yes, yes, no, no—
while each yes draws me farther from my mind's desire?

Impossibly to the north the white alp of Idea
rises up from the body's jungle. Oh, to sit
within its Cartesian snows, while the fierce cold
seduces the body toward sleep. But ever wakeful

the tongue needs only to speak and my body,
its lackey, leaps to its command: feet
at its service, hands at its service, while
the mind despairs in its tower, and its lower cousin,

tongue of my groin, hungers to lap and lap
at the sexual world like a cow at a salt lick.
Envy the mannequins poised in shop windows
not torn forward nor back by tongue, prick or mind;

envy the statues in the park. But perhaps
these too hunger in so many directions at once
that indecision has reduced them to immobility,
as if even the final paralysis of one's passing

sprung from a similar uncertainty, as if death
were just the failure to make up one's mind,
as if that failure were actually wished for
as the only escape from impossible desire,

*   *   *

the entire organism choosing its own conclusion:
mind not beaten, body not beaten, sexuality
still ascendent, embracing the compromise
that elevates death as the inevitable draw.

RECEIVERS OF THE WORLD'S ATTENTION

It is the shoes that show the breaking point,
the complete collapse in their lives, the moment
when something just whacked them and after that

all became different. You have seen these shoes
singly or in pairs, isolated in intersections,
nestling by curbs on suburban streets, bordering

expressways or by the edge of a dirt road
in Montana or Maine, maybe on a sidewalk, even
hanging from overhead wires, a pair of sneakers

suspended from blue sky like a bird transfixed
smack in the air, sometimes a shiny black brogan,
sometimes a gym shoe missing its laces. Innocuous,

innocent, the only evidence that something
peculiar has happened. And you think of a person
who has stared at the newspaper for too long,

or has gotten too wrapped up with the news on TV,
or has spent too long listening to people
complaining about It, it being the world

and all its depredations: killings here,
famines there, the usual violent mumbo jumbo,
except these people have gotten stuck in that

cul de sac where they can't push it back
like the rest of us, can't buy a new sweater
or dress and say, Boy, I sure needed that,

*   *   *

and let the world slide off a little, give them
some room to swing their arms before the pictures
crowd in again: the face of someone screaming,

the ever increasing numbers of the dead
nudging ever closer, until there occurs
an explosion inside them, some kind of attack,

and all you know is this shoe in the roadway,
this smidgin of evidence that something for somebody
went wrong. How lucky that it hasn't happened

to you yet, that the world remains distant
and abstract, hasn't overwhelmed you yet,
that your shoes are still accounted for.

But for them something snapped. Then they were
picked up, patched back together and packed off
to heal themselves. Perhaps these are the people

you see in the malls sitting hour after hour,
watching the crowds file past, the endless
buying and selling. Someone drops them off

in the morning and picks them up at night.
Sometimes they sip tea from styrofoam cups
or nibble a hot dog or thin slice of pizza.

Sometimes they form part of the crowd watching
the baton twirling display or karate display
or some fellow showing off a vegetable scraper.

*   *   *

They are eager to return to us, become
part of us again, and they sit in the mall
as a place blessedly lacking past or future:

no one dies there, the world does not intrude there.
They almost feel like people again. No one
weeps there, no one gets angry, no one

yells at them or finds fault with them or tells them
to do something quick. They sit in their new shoes
studying the crowds and trying to fix themselves,

like trying to invent a new kind of smile,
an upside-down one or sideways like a scar.
And they sit very quietly because they know

if they jump or move quickly they will break apart
and the custodians in their gray coveralls
will gather around these broken fragments of glass

with a little water, a little ice like a spilled drink
and even their spirits will be yelled at, even
their tentative souls. So they just watch

and try to believe in a world like this one:
no extremes of sound or color, no extremes
of emotion, everything exactly in the middle,

and no death, no death anyplace, and no cruelty.
And sometimes it works, sometimes they truly
get better. You can wait in the parking lot

*   *   *

and might see a man toddling out through the exit,
his arms raised for balance, taking one step
then another, blinking into the bright light,

flinching a little at the sound of traffic.
If you shouted right now you could break him.
But who wants to do that? Isn't this when

you should hurry to welcome him, to embrace him?
Wouldn't he do the same for you if your positions
were reversed and you were the one creeping back

into the world? And they are glad to be back
if only for a short time, glad for the chance
to chuckle with their families and glance around

with wonder, to reenter their passionate stories
before the world again rears up and entangles them
with the statistics of its victims, enfolds them

with all the faces of the lost, before the world
wraps its string around them and sets them spinning
between one curb and the other, while behind them

as souvenirs of the world's attention—
a black running shoe, a torn cowboy boot,
a new black pump with the heel snapped off.

THE CHILDREN

In the evening the couples came down
from the hotel. It was summer and just past
sunset. They walked along the river,
the women in long dresses, the men
in light-colored suits, while on the patio
a boy played Scarlatti on the piano.
The couples stood at the edge of the water
and breathed deeply and looked to where
the sky had grown all red in the west.
They were like deer or small animals
that come to the edge of the pasture
in early evening and sniff the air.
But the forest is deep, the silence
is deep, and from this distance they appear
as an arrested gesture, a hand caught
in the very moment of waving goodbye.
We their children keep their memory,
for what it is worth, for where we live
the air is filled with a metallic clatter
and the confusion of our own harsh cries.
From across the water, we see how
the sloping lanes are deserted, the hotels
are deserted. We were their future
and we have erased them from this earth.

BONEYARD

These people in the future won't be like us.
Oh no, they'll be kinder and their foreheads
will bulge past their noses with wisdom. They'll
have our pictures of course, although they won't
be snapshots as we know them but little
holographs, three-dimensional photos,
so when one takes one from his pocket it will look
like a miniature twentieth century person
is standing smack in the center of his palm.
There they are, they'll say kindly, the old
murderers, old child beaters, and they'll laugh
affectionately as one might laugh at a foolish eccentric
who knocks his head against a wall or takes a hammer
and again and again slambangs his own foot.
Then they'll put us in their pockets
and stroll off hand in hand. There won't
be many of them of course. They'll just
be coming back, like trees come back
after a fire, first the green shoots
like a green rug over the burned place,
then a few isolated saplings rising above
the charred logs, until the whole mountain
is covered with a new family of trees—
box elder and cedar, maple and jack pine—
and only in dark corners will there be traces
of the rich and wonderfully verdant forest
which existed a few brief heartbeats before,
black stumps, blackened foundations,
flat stones with people's names cut into them.

THE DAY THE WORLD ENDS

El día del fin del mundo . . .
yo grabaré mis iniciales
en la corteza de un tilo
sabiendo que eso no sirve para nada.
—JORGE TEILLIER

The day on which the world ends will
of course be different in each place.
Here it is raining, there snowing.
Here the night shields the now inconsequential
designs of the thief, there the sun
caressing the back of a man on the beach
begins the burn which will never keep him
awake and tossing and cursing his foolishness.
Some people are laughing, some watch a train go by.
It is surprising how many at that precise moment
are eating an apple, brushing their teeth, looking off
at a cloud that resembles a dog's head, remembering
their childhood. And in one window a hand appears.
It is sunset and the sky full of promise.
The hand, a woman's, seems almost rich
in its pinkness and plumpness; oh,
what a wealth it contains as it catches
the ring, drags down the already forsaken shade.

EXPANSION SLOTS

The ground lies muddy and dark down here
in the cemetery expansion lot where we have come
for a picnic on this first warm Sunday in March,
and now, having finished our tuna sandwiches
and *New York Times,* we curl up for a nap or,
if we can't sleep, we mean to contemplate
the mystery of life. Out on the street
stroll the folks who will someday fill these slots,
forming an additional subdivision of the dead,
but this afternoon, with sun and cloudless sky,
the weather is all they have ever wanted
as they wash their cars, go for walks or simply
drive around, radios cranked up, windows cranked down.
Maybe it's that elderly lady with her cane
and little white dog who'll occupy the spot
I'm right this moment sitting on, or perhaps
it's that creepy poetry critic from Harvard
(oh, why can't he die right away?)
or maybe it's even mine, the hole I'll call
my home. This field of struggling grass
where kids fly kites as their parents snooze
or read the paper, this field is our future.
Side by side, packed like dominoes in a box,
there's room here for another thousand more:
people who even as I ponder are pursuing
their lives with vigor and abandon, digesting
their lunches, building piles of excrement
in their innards, producing sperm, moving toward
or away from ovulation, taking little naps,
looking at the sky and wondering, wondering
what makes it all possible. Endless appetite?

Love or meanness? Money or power? How brave
to keep trudging forward with this
muddy field as their only destination.
How optimistic and pointedly forgetful.
Overcome by fellow feeling, I wish I could
jump to my feet and address them directly,
wishing them happiness and good fortune,
sweet dreams and sweeter things to eat.
And I think of that great Turkish poet,
the linear one, the straightforward one,
the one the Harvard poetry critic would despise,
and how he ended his last poem shortly before
his own death in Moscow at the age of sixty-one—
My friends, I wish you all long lives.

SLIPPING AWAY

It could be like one of those dreams
where you must carry water in your hands
for half a mile to put some fire out
and it all drips away through your fingers.

Is this forgetfulness, the world slipping away,
while confusion expands, eating our memories
like a lava flow demolishing a landscape,
thoughts like rabbits baked in their holes?

Here comes my best friend, old what's his name.
And where was that place where I first
made love and who was that girl, the one
I swore ever to be true to? The mind

like a blank screen after the film is over,
the body like the derelict in the front row
and no place to go. The mind like
frozen blue sky in the dead of winter,

the body like the shaven snow-covered fields.
But wasn't this our desire,
the destruction of past and future,
the ability to read the same page

of a book over and over and each time
we chuckle and feel amused—nothing back there
to depress one, nothing ahead to hide from,
the single moment caught like the single

*   *   *

syllable the stutterer is stuck upon,
or the record caught in a single groove
repeating a few organ notes of Bach forever?
But not forever, only until something

lifts the needle and then comes the silence,
the huge one hanging like a banner
between the light and the dark,
and across it is printed whose name?

THE BODY'S WEIGHT

A bookcase has its books, a horse supports its rider,
but the body's greatest burden is itself,
which it bears through the long day, fallen

from bed, pointed toward bed, as if the body
were the bed's creature, which the bed releases
in the morning much as a farmer turns a cow

out to pasture, summoning it back at night.
But the weight of the body—the skin settled
upon flesh and the flesh upon muscle

and the muscle upon bone; the weight
of the stomach and hips, kidneys and lungs—
all this the body carries with it,

at first lightly, eager to get started,
then gladly, scarcely knowing it is there,
a bag of feathers, a silk scarf, but then,

like a naked man rooted before a mirror,
the body is introduced to the body,
and the body begins to instruct the body—

the legs begin to feel heavy, breasts feel heavy,
the back won't straighten, belly flops forward,
the neck stiffens, arms stiffen, shoulders stiffen,

even the fingers hate to bend, and creak
like the hinges of heavy doors, while the heart
curls up in its cage like a dying spider.

*   *   *

It is then that the whispering begins,
at first not even heard, rather sensed or felt,
like a vibration deep inside us, a shivering:

Put it down, something says, put it down.
We begin to sit more and lie down more,
and the sudden inexplicable pains come more often.

It is here that the weight of the body
becomes almost a comfort, like the weight
of a hand coaxing us to rest, even though

we want to keep going; and each day the hand
presses more firmly and all gets heavier,
as if an old man, even when thin and muscular,

bears four times the weight of a young one,
as if the weight of the whole were four, six,
ten times greater than the sum of its parts;

and each day our steps get more difficult,
as if the feet were being pressed into the dirt,
so that if the ground were soft, the body

would slide through its folds like a clothespin
being pushed into powder. How did I ever manage
anything so heavy? Is it true that I once rushed

through the day with the weight of the body
as trifling as a sweater tossed over my shoulder?
Put it down, says the voice, put it down.

*   *   *

And as the daily body is the bed's creature,
so the lifely body is the earth's creature,
which is where the weight of the body

is persistently urging us, pushing us toward
the single door through which we all must exit,
till at last we pass through it and stand released

and briefly we're embraced by a joyful lightness,
as light as smoke rising, or a phrase of music,
or butterfly wings, and then the darkness begins.